NORTHERN STARS
A CHARTIST JOURNEY

NORTHERN
STARS

A CHARTIST JOURNEY

LAURENCE COCKCROFT

ILLUSTRATED BY JULIET BREEZE

Matador
9 Priory Business Park,
Wistow Road, Kibworth Beauchamp,
Leicestershire. LE8 0RX
Tel: 0116 279 2299
Email: books@troubador.co.uk
Web: www.troubador.co.uk/matador
Twitter: @matadorbooks

ISBN 978 1789015 874

Illustrated by Juliet Breeze
British Library Cataloguing in Publication Data.
A catalogue record for this book is available from the British Library.

Printed and bound in Great Britain by 4edge Limited
Typeset in 12pt Adobe Garamond Pro by Troubador Publishing Ltd, Leicester, UK

Matador is an imprint of Troubador Publishing Ltd

In memoriam
Bob Suttcliffe
William Holt
Two great Todmorden visionaries

CONTENTS

LIST OF ILLUSTRATIONS

FOREWORD

This book has been a labour of love for more than twenty-five years, since I first told the story to my older children (Jasmine and Jacob) in about 1992. They suggested I write it down; the part-time writing took many months and the 'research' included a walk with them in stormy weather over Kinder Scout as described in the book. The format changed and my youngest son, Joshua, and I worked on a new Chapter 1 together in 2000. In 2014, I was fortunate enough to meet a very talented illustrator, Juliet Breeze, who understood the spirit of the whole story from beginning to end and produced the illustrations which are now in each chapter of the book.

I was born in Todmorden, the starting point for

the march, and was raised on stories of the Industrial Revolution and in particular of the Chartists who gathered at the Basin Stone, a rock high on the moors which my father took me past many times, never omitting to say that this is where the Chartists met. They always seemed real, just as they were in a memorable painting of a meeting at the Stone, which still hangs in Todmorden's Town Hall. Todmorden's pioneering industrialist, John Fielden, was also a Chartist and as a Radical MP laid out the Petition in support of the Charter in the House of Commons in 1839, a step he saw as part of his fight for the Ten Hours Act, which was only achieved in 1847.

Ruth and Joshua Midgeley, stalwarts of the march and of numerous adventures en route, are of course fictitious, but I believe represent the world of children caught up in times of major change, as I have witnessed elsewhere in the world.

In the course of the original 'research' for the book, I read several of the substantial histories of Chartism which give us a very lively sense of what happened, and in particular of the role of the charismatic Feargus O'Connor, the publisher of the hugely popular Northern Star newspaper, every edition of which can be accessed in the British Library and which was the most important source for the book. I am grateful to all those who, when hearing of the book, have cheered me on, and in particular those who found the time to read it at various stages. In particular, I am grateful to Linda Croft, an expert on Chartism in Todmorden, and to Jeff Kaye, for his serious and thoughtful comments based on his own research into the subject. Needless to say, the events in the book are a mixture of fact and fiction but are anchored in the events of the time.

Laurence Cockcroft
September 2018

CHAPTER 1

TAKE THA' MONEY!

*Todmorden, on the border
of Lancashire and Yorkshire,
1839*

Dickie Hardwood and Joshua Midgeley stood on the cotton bale as the crane operator prepared to lift it from the canal barge to the warehouse door of Woodhouse Mill. The crane jutted from the top floor of the mill thirty yards over the canal, and was controlled by a capstan inside the warehouse. This was driven by the five men that worked in the mill, which otherwise depended on a hundred children aged between ten and fifteen.

The *Annie Maud* was a day late, and the bargeman and his family wanted to unload as quickly as possible.

Woodhouse Mill in Todmorden was the last stop on their journey on the Rochdale Canal, and they needed to return to Manchester or lose the Rochdale Canal Company's freight for a week. The bales of raw cotton which they carried had been packed in the town of Natchez, Mississippi, carried on gigantic barges on the Mississippi River to New Orleans, transferred to oceangoing freighters which carried them to Liverpool and then moved to the barges which plied the canals from Liverpool to Manchester and eventually to Rochdale and Todmorden. The bales were generally tightly sewn canvas bags, but sometimes the stitches fell apart, and the cotton burst in all directions. This cold morning was such a day.

Each bale was lifted off the boat at a shout from the bargee, with Dickie and Joshua standing on it. They were supposed to ensure that the strain of the lifting did not break the stitches on the canvas, and this required them to be hoisted up with each bale. On this occasion, Dickie was exhausted from having to work till midnight under torchlight. He overlooked the fact that two stitches of the bale were broken. As the crane lifted the bale, the stitches began to unravel, the canvas loosened, Dickie could no longer hold his position, and the cotton spilled everywhere. He was edged off the bale and plunged to the towpath thirty yards below.

His closest friends in the mill were Joshua Midgeley

and his older sister, Ruth. Ruth watched as the empty bale climbed upwards with Joshua beside it. Dickie was still lying on the towpath, nursing his leg.

Dickie plunges to the towpath.

It took another two hours before the rest of the bales were lifted. Joshua stood on each of them but was no longer watched by Ruth and the rest of the children, who had been sent back to work. Dickie Hardwood had not been able to climb the stairs to the first floor, where most of the children were working. For the time being, he rested by the boiler at the back of the mill.

The working hours of the mill were six in the morning to six in the evening on weekdays, and to five in the evening on Saturdays. The last half-hour of work on Saturdays was given over to the payment of wages for the previous week. Most of the children took home about one shilling and sixpence. The wages of two children could keep a family in food and fuel for the next week.

The accident had happened on a Thursday. On the following Saturday, when wages were due to be paid, his father, John Hardwood, appeared at Woodhouse Mill to claim those due to Dickie. This was one of the few times in the week when the owner of the mill, Jeremiah Stansfield, emerged from his office to supervise his clerk. On this occasion, he was surprised to see John Hardwood at the end of the line, cap in hand.

'I'm 'ere to claim our Dickie's wages,' said John. ''E's mending well enough, but 'e'll not be back for a couple of weeks, I reckon.'

Stansfield looked sombre. 'Your lad failed on Thursday and cost me a good five pounds. I'll tak 'im back, but I'll dock every wage of 'is until 'e's repaid those five pounds.'

John Hardwood looked shattered. 'Tha'd not do that, Mr Stansfield. Dickie's only one in't family working, and we'll never get by.'

''Ow many of your family are out of work is not my business. I don't make the rules 'ere to break them for folk like you. Tha'd best be gone.'

Hardwood had been thinking rapidly. It could take Dickie two years to pay off the five pounds. His family's wretched poverty would become even worse. Feeling bitter, he opened the challenge to Stansfield.

'If that's so, Mr Stansfield, then thou won't see me nor Dickie again – and I'll see you and your lot damned before any of my lot is back.' He crammed his hat back on his head and marched out of the mill. All the mill children were aghast, knowing the consequences for any family losing a child's wage. A good half of them were in the same position, and all were terrified of losing their jobs. However, Jeremiah Stansfield's proposals were more unjust than any which they had yet experienced. Ruth was the first to speak.

'Mr Stansfield, Dickie weren't to blame. 'E and the rest of us was 'ere till midnight last night to get them warps off. 'E was fagged out and didn't see the stitches.'

Taken aback, Stansfield was angrier than ever. 'I'll be the judge of that, and if you go on like that, lass, you'll be gone too.'

Bobby Sandsmith, a small, lively boy, joined in:

''Ow would it be, Mr Stansfield, if we all stood for Dickie and you took the five pounds off each of us wages in bits like?' Stansfield knew that this would not work because he changed at least a quarter of his child workers every year – 'to keep the others 'ungry for work,' as he put it. But it seemed a good idea to Ruth, and she tried to guess what the others were thinking. Looking around the room, she sensed that most of the children wanted to support this.

'I think you'll find we're all for it, Mr Stansfield.'

'I'm not asking thee or anyone else,' he replied. 'And you needn't come back next week; I'm done with you.'

Even Jeff Stubbs looked taken aback, knowing that Ruth was one of the best workers in the mill. But he didn't have the courage to question Stansfield's decision. Ruth was shocked at her own words. Joshua wondered how long it would be before it would be remembered that he was Ruth's brother and whether he would then be thrown out of work too. Life at their cottage at Oldroyd would take a rapid turn for the worse.

Stansfield's clerk took a walk along the line paying out the wages, and recording payments against names. As he walked down the line, he spoke the name of each boy or girl. Ruth was standing next to Bobby

Sandsmith. The clerk called out, 'Sandsmith, Bobby. Midgeley, Ruth. Midgeley, Joshua.'

Stansfield's face darkened. Jeff Stubbs, who knew Joshua was useful on the crane, looked nervous.

'Well, I'm damned,' said Stansfield. 'I near forgot that were your brother. 'E can go too. I'll 'ave none of your cheek in this mill. Now I remember; your father is a troublemaker. Led a strike at Lumbutts Mill five years ago, didn't 'e?'

Joshua was proud of the fact that his father had brought all the workers at Lumbutts Mill out in protest at the dangerous machinery there (after a man had lost an arm) and had been forced to fall back on handloom weaving as a result.

''E did, Mr Stansfield, and we've been the poorer for it since then.'

'Well, you can join 'im on 'is 'andloom then. I'll 'ave no more of you 'ere. Give 'im 'is wage,' he said to the clerk, 'and that will be the last 'e gets.'

Suddenly the whole room was silent. Ruth and Joshua looked each other in the eye with dismay. How would their parents take this disaster? Jess, their father, had not only led a strike, but was well known as a supporter of the Chartists, the new movement pressing for the total reform of Parliament by one man one vote. Although their mother had always been a supporter of Jess, she held the purse strings and exercised severe thrift. All the income Jess made from his handloom

7

was handed over to her – though this was usually no more than the combined wages of the children. They knew she would be angry and distressed.

The other mill children stood in reluctant silence – dismayed by Stansfield but too afraid to speak. Jeff Stubbs thought of speaking up for Joshua but decided against it; he'd been out of work for a year till the previous October.

Ruth held Joshua's gaze for a moment and sensing his support, nodded to him. She said, 'Tha' can keep tha' wage, Mr Stansfield, and thee'll never see us again.'

With that, she and Joshua turned on their heels and walked out of the door.

The clerk for a moment lost his composure. 'Nay, you two come back,' he said. 'Tha' mother and father will never forgive you.' But it was too late.

The two children idled home, no longer so sure that they had done the right thing. But in twenty minutes, they were home. Their mother was in the kitchen trying to stoke up the stove to a heat where it was warm enough to cook on, using as little peat as possible. The clack of the loom upstairs told them that their father was still working. The children had agreed that it would be Joshua who delivered the bad news, but that was easier said than done. Both of the children sat on the spare loom bench in the corner. Their mother, Ellen, could see that they were strangely silent.

'What's up then? Tha' doesn't look 'appy.'

'Mam, we lost us jobs.' Ruth kicked Joshua because they had agreed he would say they had rejected this week's wage at the same time. 'And we've brought nowt 'ome this week.'

Because she trusted them and sensed this was a complicated story, Ellen called up to Jess, 'Tha'd best come down, luv. Childer are back, and summut's up!'

The loom fell silent as Jess came down the ladder that led to the upper storey.

'What's wrong with you two then?' he said casting an appraising eye at Ruth and Joshua.

'They've lost their jobs. *And* there's no wage for this week,' said Ellen reprovingly. Jess looked at the children with an enquiring glance. Ruth told them the whole story, finishing with their rejection of the wage.

'Tha' young fools,' said Ellen, 'we'll scarce 'ave enough to eat in this 'ouse for next week. Never mind next month and beyond.'

'Nay, Ellen,' said Jess, 'that damn Stansfield's not fit to employ one child, let alone 'an 'undred. They did right.'

The children looked expectantly at their parents, thinking that there would be a big argument. It didn't happen: the news was too dire and involved all of them. Nobody spoke, though with a bitter look, Ellen returned to try to breathe life onto the dying fire. Jess sat down at the table and said:'You've done right, but we're in for 'ard times. Men like Stansfield need to be forced to offer better conditions or we'll be sent to gaol. Sooner or later, Parliament's got to tak men like 'im in and Fielden 'ere in Todmorden 'as got the right idea, but there are not many like 'im.'

'Finish tha' speech, Jess, and 'elp us 'ere,' said Ellen. 'Words'll not put pies on the table.'

'Is that what we're 'aving, Mam?' asked Ruth, hopefully.

'Aye, but don't blame me if this is the last for I don't know 'ow long.'

The meal they took an hour later was a silent ritual, till Jess volunteered: 'There'll be a need for one meal less tomorrow, Ellen. Feargus O'Connor 'imself is speaking at a meeting of Chartists on't market. I'll be there for three 'ours or more.'

Ruth and Joshua looked at each other, sure that they shared the same idea.

CHAPTER 2

THE BIG MEETING

Over at the open market, where the River Calder which rises on the Lancashire side of the Pennines turns east to flow into Yorkshire, a crowd of several hundred had already assembled. They were very close to a towering newly built railway viaduct which had not yet seen a train. Most of the men wore rough cloth caps, and open waistcoats or jackets over linen shirts, with leather clogs on their feet. The women – young and old alike – wore black shawls cast over their heads, with dark-coloured blouses and shirts beneath them. It was a Sunday afternoon and a good time for a meeting. There was no sign of rain, and most people would rather be out in the open than crowded into small houses and shacks with too many brothers, sisters and children.

Joshua and Ruth ran down a path along the canal to join the crowd at the marketplace. When they arrived, a tall, handsome man with full side whiskers was already speaking to the crowd in a rich Irish accent:

Feargus O'Connor at the Big Meeting.

'Are we dogs or people?' he cried. 'You work for twelve hours a day, and so do your nine-year-old children, and what for? To feed the masters and their families, not yourselves. What can you do with six shillings a week if you've got three bairns and an old grandmother to feed? And that's just when you're in work, remember three years ago in 1836 when there was no work for six months?'

Joshua and Ruth did remember, for they had already been working at Edward Heathcote's mill for one year in 1836, aged nine and eight, when the mill had been closed for six months.

'How many of you had any money coming in at all then?' shouted the speaker. 'In some of your houses, only the children were working – and when their wages were stopped, you'd nothing to eat but nettle broth, and nothing to warm yerselves with but what peat you could scratch from the moors.'

Here, a murmur of approval went up from the crowd, who remembered that bleak winter only too well. The two children remembered it too: after October, they were permanently hungry and hardly had the strength to drag themselves onto the moor to dig for peat.

'And did the masters take pity on you?'

'Aye, Fielden did,' came a cry from the crowd.

'We know Fielden's a friend of the working man,' said the speaker, 'but what about the rest of them in

Todmorden? I hear some of the big farmers, such as they call the freeholders of Langfield Common, sent their minders with dogs to chase off the peat diggers. But you can be sure they want you to work for 'em as soon as their mills have got some business.'

Joshua felt his ankle. It was healed now, but there had been a great scar there for nearly a year, where a hunting dog had caught him as he and six other men and lads had fled before the gamekeeper's pack.

'No, my friends, this will never do in Todmorden; never do in Yorkshire; never do in England. How many here fought at Waterloo?'

Six men raised their hands; one standing on a crutch, for he had lost a leg to Napoleon's gunners.

'What did you fight for, lads? To stop Boney and those Frenchies who were so easy with the guillotine. And what did you get for stopping 'im? Why, in Lancashire alone, thirty thousand little bairns must go to work to feed their mothers and fathers. And who can speak for the working father, mother or child when Parliament is for the masters only, never mind our Reform Act, and most of them is handpicked by their lordships.

'It's a vote for every man we want. And a new Parliament to be elected every year, and every town to send its own member.'

Here the crowd shouted its approval. 'All this, my friends, is in our Charter.' And here the speaker's helpers unfolded a great scroll, held between two pieces of wood, with the six demands written in bold characters:

ONE MAN ONE VOTE
VOTE BY BALLOT
ANNUAL PARLIAMENTS
NO PROPERTY QUALIFICATION
EQUAL REPRESENTATION
PAYMENT FOR MPs

Like most of the crowd, Ruth and Joshua could not read, and a Parliament far away in London didn't mean much to them but they knew that their families were badly treated and that somebody must be able to speak for them.

'Lads and lasses, it's a million signatures we want,' cried the speaker. 'And every one of them to go to Parliament in London to let them know that the people must be heard. And to let me know that there are hundreds of thousands that's not afraid of redcoats or prisons. How many of you will sign here today?'

Here, his assistants began to unravel an enormous roll of paper which was already covered with signatures and the signs of those who could not write. It was far from a million but could be numbered in many hundreds of thousands.

'Now come forward and fight to better yerselves, for no one else will do it for you. The Charter's the best hope you've got.'

A trickle of people came forward from the crowd and were given feather quills to write with. Those who could not write made a sign with the pen, and the speaker's helpers wrote their names for them.

But the numbers were not enough.

'Where's your courage, lads? There's not a redcoat in sight, and I doubt that London's got its spies in *this* place – to be sure, they think you don't know what a vote is here!'

Moved to show they were not so ignorant, nearly two hundred of the crowd moved forward to sign the Charter. Joshua and Ruth saw their father join the line.

'Now, lads,' cried O'Connor, 'we're going to march from Manchester to London next month to put the Charter to Parliament directly and if they won't see us, we'll go to her Majesty herself. It'll be a long, tough march, starting outside Manchester and going on through Nottingham, where they're all for the Charter. We need every man we can get, aye, and women and children too if you can spare 'em. Now, who here will join us?'

About twenty of the crowd put their hands in the air, but as the speaker called for more, Joshua and Ruth saw their father, Jess Midgeley, join them. They stared at each other in astonishment.

'What'll me mam say?' said Ruth.

'She'll never let 'im go,' cried Joshua.

'I'd want to go too, Joshua,' said Ruth.

'What, you!' said her brother. 'You walk to London… tha'd never get as far as Manchester.'

'You wait,' said Ruth. 'Just wait and see.'

As their dad turned back to the crowd after signing the petition, he saw the two children, who by this time had wormed their way to the edge of the crowd. He hurried over to them crying:

'This is no place for the likes of you two. Get 'ome to yer mam or there'll be no tea for you today.'

'Why shouldn't we be 'ere?' cried Ruth. 'If we can work in Stansfield's mill, we can support t'Charter.'

'That's enough,' said Jess Midgeley. 'No more o' that from you,' and taking the hands of both children, he walked them firmly away from the crowd.

The Midgeleys' cottage lay in a row of cottages at Oldroyd, about a mile from the marketplace where the meeting had been held. From its windows, you could see a sloping field and the canal, and the River Calder running alongside it. Behind the cottage, the hill rose more steeply; first through woods, and then to open fields and then onto the moor where they had dug for peat. If you stood outside the cottage and looked to the east, you could see the tall column of Stoodley Pike, a monument built to peace with the French after the long war.

In summer, the scene was often fair, although the steam engines which most of the mills now used were belching out smoke so that the air was never really clear. In winter, the scene was nearly always dismal: dark clouds hung over the hills, and Joshua and Ruth went to work before six o'clock in the dark, and returned at eight o'clock in the evening when it had already been dark for nearly four hours. In winter, Sundays were the only days when they saw their house in daylight.

On this Sunday, as they walked up the hill towards the house with their father, they could see their mother, Ellen, standing anxiously in the doorway. For years now, she had looked pale and drawn, partly from the long hours she worked herself when there was work, and partly from concern for Ruth and Joshua. The mill life was new to her – as a child, she had lived high up on the moor at her father's farm, and run wild amongst the heather and sheep. But her father had been forced to abandon the farm; the family had moved to the valley bottom, and he and Ellen's mother had taken work in the first big cotton mills. They had found the change unbearable, and both had died within five years.

When Ellen married Jess, it was her greatest delight that they could rent a cottage set at least a little way up the hill but her greatest sorrow was that the children would never run free as she had done.

'Why, where 'ave you been?' she cried, as Jess and the children returned to the cottage. 'Yer late for yer tea.'

'Well, I'm late for good reason,' said Jess, still holding both children by the hand. 'But why these two are late is another question.'

'We were on 't 'market, mam,' said Joshua, 'and there were a big meeting wi'that big Irishman, what's called Feargus O'Connor. There were 'undreds there. An' O'Connor were calling for t'Charter, an' 'e wants a million people to sign it.'

'Well, 'e wouldn't get many in this town, we're that ground down,' said Ellen.

'Hundreds signed,' said Ruth, 'and Dad were one of 'em.'

Jess Midgeley looked sheepish.

'You did what, Jess Midgeley?' said Ellen.

'Wait on, if nobody comes forward, we'll soon 'ave all 't 'childer in this country working in 't 'mills, and dying afore they're twenty. O'Connor's rough but 'e's right. I'd no choice, Ellen. Besides, Fielden's wi'em right enough.'

'Yes,' said Ruth, 'of course Dad were right – and 'e should be on 't 'march to London.'

'March to London!' said Ellen. 'What march?'

'To give t'Charter 't 'Parliament men, Mam,' said Joshua, 'and to let 'em know that what's 'appening in 't 'country'.'

'Ellen, they're right,' said Jess. 'I should be there.'

'*You* walk to London!' said Ellen. 'It'd tak you nigh on a year.'

'But we've got to act, Ellen. You want yer grandchildren to be starting work afore six too?' said Jess.

''E's right, Mam. 'E must go, and Joshua and I should go too – folk in London don't just need to 'ear about us childer what are in 't 'mills – they need to see us.'

'But what about your jobs? You'll lose 'em.'

'Well, you won't 'ave to feed us while we're away, and you've got some money coming in from Crossley's sewing shop.'

Ruth looked appealingly to her father, who realised that the Chartists needed children to march with them. But he knew too that the three shillings per week that Ellen earned would not go far, and how lonely she would be if they left her on her own.

'Let them come, Ellen,' he said quietly. 'They'll 'ave to fight for themselves in life one day, and they might as well start now. Anyway, it'll be no 'arder than 'Eathcote's mill before six.'

Ruth and Joshua looked amazed. Was their dad really agreeing they could march too? And to London?

Their mother looked helpless. She could never win against the three of them.

'When would you start?' she said limply.

'It won't be till next month,' said Jess. 'There'll be a big meeting outside Manchester and then the march will begin. We'll 'ear the date soon enough.'

'It'll be October,' she said. 'You'll freeze to death o'nights. I'll 'ave to make you two clothes o'that blanket.'

'So you'll agree, Mam?' said Ruth.

'Only because I must.'

The children ran to her and hugged her, while Jess Midgeley looked at them smiling – and wondered if they really would reach London and Parliament.

CHAPTER 3

GATHERING STRENGTH

It was a rare clear autumn morning when they left, with the sun creeping over the moor's edge. As Joshua and Ruth came to the door, they could look up and see the hills bathed in a soft light, and look below and see the pall of smoke through which they normally walked to work.

'Wish you were going to work, Josh?' said Ruth.

'No fear,' said her brother. 'But I'll miss Jim that I pull 't 'trolley with.'

'Well, we should find other children on 't 'march, and I'll be glad to be well away from t'mill. I 'ate it.'

'Well, I'm glad it's not forever,' said Joshua. 'I want to see this place again.'

Their mother called them inside to give them the coats she'd made from their only blankets. Their father would carry a cloth bag with bread and cheese which would have to last them their first day's march to Manchester. After that, they were to depend on the goodwill of the Chartist supporters on the route to London.

'Well, we 'ave to be going, lass,' said Jess to his wife, putting on a brave face.

Ellen could hardly bear to look at her children, now grey and lumpy in their blanket-coats. But their faces were brave and she knew they wanted to go.

'Well, go then,' she said quietly, 'but for God's sake, come back.' She clasped the children to her, but a minute later they broke away as their father called them to the door.

'See you in a month Mam,' they cried as they followed their father down the path to the town. Ellen watched them go and wondered if it would not be longer than that.

Jess Midgeley had arranged to meet the other marchers from Todmorden at the market by the River Calder where they had heard Feargus O'Connor speak. About a dozen other men had volunteered to join the march, nearly all of them out of work. Only six were ready for the march when Jess and the children arrived. Their gruff "Good mornings" masked the respect they had for Jess, who was known to be a man ready to speak up for others. But they looked doubtfully at Ruth and Joshua, worried that they might hold them up.

'Nay, Jess, tha's not bringin' childer as well as tha' self?' said a big man with clogs and a twisted walking stick, who looked as though he might kick or beat the children off the march anytime.

'I am that, Ralph Murphy – we want them Parliament men to meet some of these childer what never see the light of a winter's day.'

'But they'll never get to Manchester, never mind London, Jess,' said Murphy, clutching his stick.

'We will n'all,' said Ruth. 'If we can work twelve hours a day year round, we can do owt you men can.'

'Mind your tongue, lass,' said Jess. 'They're coming, Ralph, and if you can get to London, so will they. Now who else are we waiting for?'

'Abraham Eastwood and Fred Dawson 'ave both been kept back by their wives, I shouldn't wonder,' said Eric Naylor, a small man whose mouth always seemed open in laughter, though he had little enough to laugh about. A man with no family, he drifted from job to job in Todmorden, cleaning out cotton waste or helping load the canal barges.

'Better to 'ave seven stout hearts and two strong childer than twelve doubting Thomases,' said Judd Ackroyd, a fit man in his forties who carried a sledgehammer over his shoulder. As a young man, he had been in the Luddite gangs which used sledgehammers to smash wool shearing machines in mills in Halifax. Whenever he felt danger might be in the air, he carried his hammer.

'Aye, tha's reet enough there, Judd,' said Jethro Strongitharm, a big dark man with one leg and a crutch. 'If we'd 'ad these two at Waterloo, we'd 'ave finished off Boney by lunchtime, and I'd 'ave me two legs.'

Jethro had fought against Napoleon at Waterloo, and in one of the last charges had lost his leg to a cannonball. In the last seventeen years, he'd eventually learned to walk with one leg and a crutch almost as fast as he marched as a soldier. 'Let 'em come. They'll get to London alreet.'

Jess Midgeley, pleased that his children had two strong supporters in the group, decided to make no more of it. 'Now, lads; where's this banner Annie Rowley's lass promised to make? Folk 'av got to know who we are and why we're marching.'

'There she is, coming up 't 'Calder,' said Jim Knotts, a sandy-haired young man of about twenty who was always ready for an adventure. The march to London was about the biggest adventure he could think of, and he was in a boisterous mood. 'That's Marion Rowley, all right,' and he ran over to welcome her.

'Let's see t'banner then, Marion,' he almost shouted at her as they met at the riverside.

'All in good time, Jim Knotts,' Marion replied in a musical voice, as they walked together back to the others. Marion was small, with dark hair tied in a bun and with a warm look to her face. She had learned sewing from her mother, Annie, who worked in the sewing shop which was part of Edward Heathcote's mill. For a time, Marion had worked there herself; but when the mill closed for six months three years previously, she'd never got her job back and had not found work anywhere else.

'Cum on, what 'ave you done for us, lass?' said Jess. 'Let's see it.'

Ruth and Joshua partly knew Marion from Sunday School outings where her singing was always the most popular event of the afternoon. On those occasions – sometimes out on the moors – the music seemed to pour out of her in a rich stream of sound, full of feeling for the hardships of the world around her.

'Hullo, Ruth and Joshua,' she cried. 'Going on a bit of a walk, are you? Better than 't 'mill anyroad. Come 'an 'elp us unfurl this banner.'

The banner was tied between two poles, each about six feet long, and the children bent down to separate the poles and stretch the banner. The black lettering had been sewn onto a four-foot square of grey cloth – of the kind which Heathcote's mill was producing at the rate of thousands of yards per month.

It read:

THE CHARTER TODAY —
OR NO WORK TOMORROW

'That'll do fine, lass,' said Jess Midgeley. 'We'll be thinking of thee then.'

'Thinking of me! I'm coming with you, and I'm ready to start now. I've got me bundle 'ere,' said Marion as she produced a knapsack in the same grey cloth from under her coat.

'Well, that caps it,' said Ralph Murphy. 'The two children and a woman – we'll not get beyond the ten miles to Rochdale.'

Marion knew Ralph as a killjoy who never clapped her singing and could be relied on to see the worst in any situation.

'Ralph Murphy, I'll 'ave you know that I walked the twenty mile to Manchester to see me Aunt Flo last week. We started at five o'clock and got there at one. I'll make it to London, don't you worry. Besides, somebody's got to keep these two warm at night,' she said, smiling at Ruth and Joshua.

The children were secretly relieved that Marion was joining them. Ruth took her hand but Joshua hung back.

'I reckon we should be glad enough for anyone who's willing to join us,' said Jess. He was glad that Marion was joining them but nervous that his little group might not hold together. But then he remembered her singing

27

and realised what a bond it could be when times were rough. 'Especially someone whose voice can be 'eard 'alf a mile away. Come on, let's go.'

The little group moved across the market square, attracting a few shouts of good luck and support – but at seven o'clock on a Monday morning, most people were bent on their own business. Ruth and Joshua took one pole of the banner, and Jim Knott the other. The small band of marchers set off behind the banner; Judd Ackroyd with his hammer and Jethro Strongitharm with his crutch, bringing up the rear.

They left the town by the gravel-topped road to Manchester that wound its way alongside the canal. Both the road and the canal were teeming with life: the road with horses and carts on local errands, the canal with barges piled high with bales of raw cotton or boxes of woven grey cloth. Joshua and Ruth had been delighted to hold the banner as they left the town. Half an hour later, the weight was beginning to tell; and they were glad when Jess Midgeley suggested that they furl up the banner until they'd covered the ten miles to Rochdale, where they expected to join the Rochdale marchers.

Five miles out of Todmorden, they could hear the crash of a giant steam hammer as it smashed stone in a nearby quarry. The children ran up to the brow of a hill to watch it at work, and were amazed at the bustling scene of activity which was taking place below them.

Hundreds of men were moving in all directions: some with wheelbarrows, some with buckets brimming over with liquid, some with sledgehammers at least as big as Judd Ackroyd's. Most of this action was centred on two lines of metal, which ran into an opening in the hill. Small trolleys were running up and down this line and disappearing into the opening which was cut from rock.

While they were staring at the scene, Jim Knotts came up behind the children:

'Never seen owt like this before, you two, 'ave you?' he said.

'What's going on?' said Ruth.

'This is 't tunnel for railway from Manchester to Leeds – and some say it's longest in 't world,' said Jim. 'They've got a thousand men working 'ere and five killed already. God knows 'ow many more will die afore they're finished.'

An engine with a cloud of steam blowing out of its chimney puffed up to the opening of the tunnel, pulling behind it an enormous pile of bricks.

'So that's one of them engines,' said Joshua.

'Aye, an' when tunnel's through all 't 'way, engines'll tak thee from Manchester to Todmorden in a bit over two hours, and from Manchester to Leeds in near enough four.'

'That'll be the way to travel,' said Joshua. 'Can you get to London that way?'

'Not yet. Tha' can only get from London to Birmingham, but that'll change soon enough.'

'Just as well,' said Jess Midgeley as he came up behind them. 'We're marching to show folk all long t' road that we've got a just cause and that we're fighting

Ruth and Joshua with Jim Knotts at the big tunnel.

tooth and nail for it. Now come on, you three, back on to 't road.'

Ruth and Joshua returned to their position in the group behind Jim Knotts, who was carrying the banner, now rolled up on its two poles and slung over his shoulder. They were followed by Marion Rowley, who wanted to keep close to the children. The others followed and Judd Ackroyd, swinging his big hammer as if to stamp out any opposition, brought up the rear.

Before midday, they were on the outskirts of Rochdale, halfway to Manchester. Jess Midgeley had been told to meet the Rochdale marchers in Toad Lane. There they would meet marchers from all the nearby cotton and wool manufacturing towns. Feargus O'Connor had been busy stirring up support for the Charter throughout this area, and marchers from at least twenty towns were expected to meet in Rochdale. As the Todmorden group came closer to the centre of town, they realised that a large crowd was thronging the streets.

'Put t'banner up, Jim,' said Jess Midgeley. 'We'll 'ave to show ourselves 'ere. Ralph, you tak t'other pole from Jim. Ruth and Joshua, stick close to Marion. Now let's walk in twos, with Judd an' 'is 'ammer at back.'

As the Todmorden group came closer to the crowd, their banner was recognised.

''Ere's one lot, cum to join our lads,' cried one.

'Where they from?' cried another.

'Looks like Tod.'

'Oh aye, cripples n'all.'

'An' a big 'ammer to keep off you an' me. Tha' can never trust folk from Tod.'

''Appen they want to keep their childer under control – look at them two.'

Ruth and Joshua realised they were being scrutinised.

'And are your children marching for 't 'Charter?' Ruth shouted at the speaker in the crowd. 'We'll get to London and back, tha' knows.'

Taken aback, the speaker disappeared into the crowd.

By now, other marching groups were converging on Toad Lane, and it was difficult for Jess Midgeley to keep his group together. 'Stick to Marion, children,' he said. 'I'm going to talk to 't' Rochdale organisers.'

Ruth and Joshua held Marion's hands as the crowd pressed around them. Some of the groups had brought musical instruments – drums, fiddles and trumpets – and a clash of different tunes filled the air as they all tried to reach Toad Lane. Marion could hardly bear to hear music without singing herself, but could now barely recognise a single tune. Some kind of order was beginning to emerge as a small man standing on a platform at the side of the square waved his hands, and was evidently trying to get the marching groups to form up behind each other.

'Come on, lads,' he cried. 'You've got to be in Manchester by tonight for 't procession by torchlight. Soldiers'll be there and we need plenty of men. We don't want another Peterloo with redcoats killing right, left and centre.'

'What does 'e mean about Peterloo?' Joshua asked Marion.

'That's twenty years ago in 1819 when t'army tore into a crowd of working folk in St Peter's Field in Manchester – just because they was demanding their rights. Me Uncle Jim were there and 'e got 'issel knocked down by a cavalry officer on an 'orse.'

Joshua looked uncertainly at Ruth; it was the first time he had thought they might meet real danger. Perhaps it would be better to be working in Stansfield's mill after all – you might be tired but you stayed alive. Ruth could sense his feelings and shared his fear but wanted to go on at all costs.

'They wouldn't do it again, surely?' she said to Marion. 'Aren't there too many of us now?'

'Aye, there should be, lass. Let's see 'ow many join us when we get to Manchester.'

The small man standing on a platform was beginning to achieve some order amongst the various groups of marchers. 'Come on, you from Bacup, you tak the second slot; you from Burnley, you're at th'end; Rawtenstall, come in the middle 'ere.'

Jess Midgeley came back to his group, and Ruth

and Joshua both ran up to him, grabbing his hands. 'What's 'appening, Dad?' cried Joshua.

'We're at the beginning, lad; and we'd better get everybody there just now.' Raising his voice, he called on the rest of the Todmorden marchers to follow him to the front of the line.

'Why choose us, Dad?' said Ruth.

'They must think we look a likely bunch with a one-legged man, two children and an 'ammer,' Jess laughed.

'You mean the soldiers wouldn't dare to charge us, like at Peterloo?' said Ruth.

'Who's been talking to you, lass?' said Jess, looking at Marion.

'I were just telling 'em what 'ad 'appened before,' said Marion.

'Well, that's a while ago anyway,' said Jess. 'Now, come on, let's get into position. We're going to form up again two mile outside Manchester, and move into the city in a torchlit march once it gets dark. That'll be by about 'alf past eight. Then an 'our later, we'll form up on St. Peters Field where there'll be speeches from some o 't' leaders.'

'Do you think we'll still be awake?' said Joshua to Ruth.

'I'll set you alight with me torch if I so much as see you nodding off,' said Ruth.

Jess led the children and the rest of the Todmorden group to the front of the march as the other groups tried to find their right places in the line. The jostling crowd, the increasing numbers of marchers, the different tunes being played by various marching groups all gave Ruth and Joshua a sense of excitement and expectation. By now, it was clear that most of the marching groups had many more than eight participants. As Jess looked back from the steps of the platform, he guessed that there were at least a thousand people trying to form a line.

'Marion, you 'old t'poles of t'banner, and you two children t'other one. When you get tired, we'll get young Jim 'ere to tak over,' Jess said, nodding at Jim Knotts.

'Right enough,' said Jim, only too happy to march alongside Marion when his chance came.

As the marchers fell into a rough line, the small man raised his voice to higher and higher levels so as to be heard.

'Now, lads,' he cried, 'we want you at Ancoats by six o'clock.' Fearing that no one had heard him, he asked a man with a bugle to blow a blast, which quietened those groups around him.

'At Ancoats by six o'clock, lads. That's when t' Manchester crowd'll 'ave your food 'n' torches ready.'

Still doubtful that more than three or four of the marching groups had heard him, he rushed with the bugler towards the back of the column and repeated his message.

'It's off with you now, lads; and good luck. You must be at Ancoats by six – only ten miles. Let's 'ave another blast on 't'bugle an' tha' can start.'

The bugler blew a long high-pitched note, and Jess Midgeley, guessing that this must be the signal for departure, called on the Todmorden group to lead off. For half an hour, Ruth and Joshua found the banner easy enough to carry. As they went further through Rochdale, they passed through a series of cobbled streets, containing both houses and workshops. In the background, there were enormous mill buildings, three or four storeys high. Gradually, the streets fell away again to low-lying green fields, but as Ruth and Joshua turned round, they could see the high moorland lying a few miles to the east.

'When will we be back there, Ruth?' asked Joshua.

'Sooner than you think, Josh,' but she wondered at the truth of her own words.

CHAPTER 4

UNDER FIRE IN MANCHESTER

When Ruth and Joshua saw the immense crowd in the fields just outside Manchester, they were amazed. Within half an hour of leaving Rochdale, they had handed over their pole which carried the banner to Marion, and trudged behind her for a full four hours. Jess Midgeley had been too busy moving back and forth along the line of marchers, talking to the other leaders, to help them. By seven o'clock in the evening, they were so tired they felt they could hardly move another step.

But now they could see that the thousand marchers from Rochdale were only one of at least twenty similar groups. Some had arrived well before the Rochdale group; others were arriving at the same time. Over on one side, beyond a stone wall, Joshua noticed a line of about a hundred horsemen in red uniform.

'Is them soldiers, Marion?' he said.

'As like as not,' said Marion, anxious that their earlier talk about Peterloo might have sapped the children's eagerness for the march.

'I'm going to talk to Jethro, wi 't'crutch,' said Joshua, dropping back in the line to the back of the Todmorden marchers.

Six lines back from the front, Jethro Strongitharm was swinging his body along, balancing his weight between his crutch and his good leg.

''Ow are you feeling, lad?' he said as Joshua made his way towards him. 'Still ready for London, or missing yer mam's tea?'

'Oh, I'm reet enough, but what about them 'orsemen over yonder?' said Joshua. 'The ones in red coats?'

Jethro glanced to the side of the enormous field into which they were now marching and could see the red and white colours of the West Riding regiment – his own regiment at Waterloo.

'Well, damn me,' he cried. 'It's our own lads that's turning on us now.'

Joshua gave him a startled look and thought he could see tears come to the old soldier's eyes. He could n 't' believe that such a tough old hero as Jethro – who seemed to be happy enough living on one leg – could be brought to tears by the sight of a line of soldiers.

'What do you mean, our own lads?' asked Joshua.

'Why, lad, them men there is from my regiment, and we were in 't'last charge on the French cannons. 'Appen not my old comrades, but their sons, like as not. And now… and now…' Joshua was sure this time that he could see a tear rolling down Jethro's cheek.

'Why, for the Duke of Wellington's own regiment to turn on us… that's more than I can bear, lad, after all we did for 'im. Charter's a just cause. They've no right to turn one soldier on another. England'll never stand for it.'

'Will they charge us then?' asked Joshua, looking up at Jethro.

'Not they, lad; ah reckon they're just there trying to scare us off. Keep your eyes on the man at front on the great white horse. If 'e's moving up and down, it means 'e's getting nervous and might do owt. If he's still, 'e's not likely to tell 'is men to move. This is a bad day; I'll not get over this, lad.'

Joshua gave him a frightened look and moved back up the line to fall in with Marion and Ruth.

'They ARE soldiers, and even Jethro's scared of 'em,' he said, not sure whether Jethro's tears bespoke fear or pain at the sight of the men of his old regiment watching the field.

'Well, there's nothing you can do about it, Josh; so just keep quiet, will you?' said Ruth as the whole of the Rochdale marching column came to a halt in the middle of the field.

They spotted another group of children sitting down about a hundred yards away and, suddenly finding new energy, walked over to see them. Coming closer, they could see that they were eating a tea laid out on grey cloth.

'Allo,' said Ruth. ''Ave you come far? Tired out yet?'

'No,' answered a red-headed boy with a lump of cheese in his mouth, 'just from Salford.'

''Ow far's that?' asked Ruth.

'About two mile.'

Ruth couldn't resist a laugh – Salford seemed so near after the twenty-mile walk from Todmorden. But the ginger-haired boy didn't like it.

'Well then, what've you got to laff about? We're all 'ere together, aren't we, Jack?'

'That's reet, Davey,' said a small boy sitting next to him, with a red handkerchief tied round his neck. 'Don't tak owt from this lot tha' wouldn't tak from Manchester lads.'

'Oh, what are you on about?' said Ruth. 'I didn't mean to laff at you. It's just that we've been walking all day, a good twenty mile, and two mile didn't seem much.'

Davey and his group calmed down at this news and asked if Ruth and Joshua had eaten.

'No, but we've got ours over there,' said Joshua, pointing back to the Todmorden group.

'Bring it over then, an' you can tell us 'ow you're still alive after these twenty mile,' said Davey.

Ruth and Joshua went over to find their father with the knapsack which their mother had carefully made up, and returned with a good handful of cheese and bread.

'That looks right good cheese,' said Davey, surprised at its whiteness.

'Try a bit,' said Ruth, handing him a part of her handful.

'Aye, I were right,' said Davey. 'This is better than we get from Mother Cross and 'er three cows in Salford, any day. But then she keeps those in what's left of a meadow by th'Irwell River, where drunks dry out of a night.'

'Well, this is from me aunt's farm at Black Clough in Todmorden,' said Ruth, 'and she makes it right crumbly.'

'Aye, it fair crumbles in yer mouth,' said Davey. 'I wouldn't mind some more o' this, eh, lads?'

'Right enough, Davey,' said the small boy Jack who had been sitting next to him, but now stood up signalling to his six fellows to do the same.

Before Ruth and Joshua knew what was happening, their chunks of cheese had been snatched from them and they found themselves pitched onto the ground.

'So that's what you Salford lads are about,' said Ruth, watching her precious tea devoured by Davey's gang. 'What shall we do about it, Josh?'

Joshua, from his vantage point on the ground, eyed the ring of boys uneasily. 'Well, I'll tak on young Jack, if 'e'll give me a fight,' said Joshua.

Jack was only too happy to test his prowess as a wrestler and came up to stand right in front of Joshua. The two boys locked arms and struggled to floor each other. Although naturally cautious, Joshua had been the best wrestler among the boys at Stansfield's mill; and before long, he and Jack were rolling on the ground with neither able to pin the other down.

Just as it seemed Joshua might gain the advantage, Marion Rawley came running over, having seen the fight begin.

'Joshua Midgeley, stop that this minute,' she said. 'You should be ashamed of yourself. We're not 'ere to fight each other. And what do you lads think yer doing?'

Davey's gang looked shamefaced as the two boys rose from the ground. 'It were the cheese,' said Davey. 'We didn't mean no 'arm.'

'Well, get back to your group,' said Marion. 'They're passing out torches now. Come on, you two.'

Ruth and Joshua walked back at Marion's side in low spirits. Ruth felt she had been cheated by Davey's gang; Joshua felt he would have beaten Jack decisively given a few more minutes. But as they approached the head of the Rochdale column, their attention was caught by the sight of a horse and cart which was now surrounded by marchers. Standing in the middle of the cart, a thickset man in a brown smock was handing out wooden sticks about two feet long. As the children came closer, they could see that each of these had small metal cups attached to one end. At the back of the cart, a man was pouring a liquid into the cups of a group standing round him.

'Come on, John, we've not got long. We've got five more lines to do yet,' said the man in the back of the cart.

'Fair enough, Josiah; but tha' doesn't want oil all over't ground, does tha'.' said his colleague.

'Can we 'ave three please?' Marion said on behalf of herself and the children. These were quickly handed to her and the children could see that each metal cup contained a wick. John, at the back of the cart, was pouring liquid pig's fat into the cups so that the wicks could light. The children joined the circle surrounding him and quickly had their cups filled.

'Can we light 'em now?' asked Joshua.

Hearing the question, Josiah, at the front of the cart, answered: 'No, lad; tha' cannot. That oil is right scarce and I wouldn't like to say 'ow we and t'other wagonners got ten gallons of it. Nobody lights up till it gets dark and we're into Manchester.'

''Ow 'igh will 't'flame rise, Marion?' asked Joshua.

'No more than a good three inches, lad; but with thousands and thousands of 'em, we'll be fit to set Manchester ablaze.'

Jess Midgeley came up behind them, anxious to make sure that all the Todmorden group had torches.

The Torchlight Procession in Manchester

'Now then, Marion, what's this? We'll 'ave no talk o'setting owt ablaze. This is a peaceful gathering, lass. We're common people claiming us rights. An' wi' them soldiers there, we'd better stick to that.'

'Aye, no burns, but a few bangs, eh, Jess?' said Judd Ackroyd, swinging his enormous hammer through the air.

'Neither of 'em, Judd. You think the lads in red'll give us 'alf a chance if there's any trouble? They'll mow us down like at Peterloo as soon as tha's got that 'ammer off tha' shoulder.'

Before Judd could reply, the word was passed round from column leaders that they should prepare to march off, with as many as possible carrying the torches. A total of nineteen columns had arrived at the Ancoats fields. Jess had heard another of the column leaders, Frank Sykes, a weaver from Oldham, estimate that there were a good twenty thousand there in all. The whole procession was nearly three miles in length. It took the Oldham column ten minutes to march out of the field, closely followed by Rochdale.

'Where do we go now, Dad?' said Ruth.

'We'll be following road down Oldham Street into centre of Manchester and fetch up at St Peter's Field, where 't'Peterloo Massacre 'appened twenty year ago. It's big and central and all kinds o'folk is there – and t'army lads'll never dare to 'arm us there after what 'appened in '19.'

'An' what'll we do when we get there?' Ruth continued.

'Three o 't'Chartist leaders and their supporters'll be there to speak. You'll 'ave seen two of 'em afore – Feargus O'Connor and John Fielden.'

'What, you mean Fielden of Waterside Mill, where me anty Leah works?'

'Aye, the same man, Ruth, and one what's fighting for more than 'is own profits and believes that working folk shouldna' toil more than ten 'ours a day. 'E's one 't'Members of Parliament for Oldham now – neither Whig nor Tory but Radical, and let's 'ope he stays so.'

'So why does Anty Leah work so long then?' persisted Ruth.

'Why, lass; Fielden can't change 'is mills' hours till t'other masters do. That's reet enough – or 'e'd never make money to fight for better times. Now get ready for off, and don't let that oil drip out o' your torch, Joshua.'

Marion, Ruth, Joshua, and Jim Knotts were still at the head of the Rochdale column. But the children were tired now and left it to Jim and Marion to hold the poles. Besides, they each had a torch in one hand and had to hold it upright.

As the Rochdale column moved out of the field, the sound of powerful male voices began to fill the air. Ruth and Joshua could hardly make out the words, but as soon as she heard the singing, Marion recognised the tune and the words. Taking them up in her rich voice, she sang the song that was a tribute to the heroes of

Peterloo, led by Henry Hunt and attacked by the police chief Nadin Joe:

"With Henry Hunt we'll go me boys,
With Henry Hunt we'll go,
We'll mount the cap of liberty,
In spite of Nadin Joe,
On the sixteenth of August eighteen hundred and
*   nineteen,*
A meeting held in Peter Street,
Was glorious to be seen.
Joe Nadin with his big bulldogs as you would
*   plainly see,*
And on the other side, stood the bloody cavalry.
From Stockport Town and Ashton,
The weaver lads came in,
Who all behaved with honour bright,
The meeting to begin,
Upon the ground they all did meet,
Like heroes of renown,
Search all the men o' th'nation,
Our match cannot be found.

Soon the song, which had been popular throughout the mill towns of Lancashire for nearly twenty years, was taken up by each of the columns as they made ready to march. Within five minutes, the song was resounding throughout the field.

Ruth and Joshua knew a few of the words but soon picked up the rest as the song was sung a second and third time. Marching out of the field and buoyed up by the singing, they regained their energy. Glancing to his left, Joshua noticed the officer at the front of the horsemen was moving up and down – the very act which Jethro had warned could be a sign of danger.

'Look at that, Ruth,' he said. 'Yon soldiers are getting bothered – they don't like this song.'

'I expect it's talk of "bloody cavalry" they don't like,' said Ruth. 'They don't like to be so unpopular. But I wouldn't panic.'

The children picked up the song again and walked just behind Marion and Jim. Now the whole three-mile line of columns was snaking out of the field and "*With Henry Hunt We'll Go*" seemed to echo to the skies, as the horses of the fusiliers nervously pawed the ground. Ruth and Joshua were swept along in the excitement of the moment, rapidly forgetting tiredness, hunger – and bruises. Joshua wondered briefly if Davey and his gang would reappear, or if they were safely sandwiched inside the Salford column.

As the line moved away from the field, it passed through a long unpaved road with ramshackle dwellings on either side. Made from timber poles, rejected quarry stones, pieces of tin and in some cases clods of earth, their 'front doors' opened onto open drains. As Ruth and Joshua marched down the street, they were amazed by how primitive the houses were and by the strength of the stench coming from the drains. It was obvious that every kind of household waste found its way into them and that they were never cleared. Even more striking were the people who stood outside the houses or lent over half doors. Ruth and Joshua, used to working from dawn till dusk and to finishing their meals hungry, nevertheless looked in disbelief at the rags which some of the boys and girls in this street were wearing – all of them gave the appearance of being ill-nourished and without energy. Though brave cries of support were shouted to the marchers as they crowded into the road, it was obvious that few people here had the spirit to join the march.

Ruth realised she was walking just in front of her dad and turned round to him. 'But, Dad,' said Ruth, 'I've never seen such a mess, or smelt such a stench. Life in Tod is bad enough, but this is a kind of 'ell.'

'Aye, Ruth; tha's reet enough, and that's one of things that's got to change. Charter'll 'elp wi' that.'

Eventually, the dusty, rutted, ill-drained road turned into a street with cobblestones and, as it did so, the quality of houses noticeably improved. Leading off the road were streets with double storey houses, painted doors and cellars reached by stone steps. Each street seemed to contain hundreds of houses, all in a line, and at the end of each one was a crowd of supporters of the march, ready to join in at the end of any of the columns.

At the end of many of the streets was a towering mill building, up to seven or eight storeys high, belching out smoke into the evening air.

It had been agreed that the torches would be lit by 8.30pm – just before dusk fell. A party of young boys with lighted tapers were running down each of the lines setting a light to every torch. Ruth and Joshua could see the torches of the Oldham column in front of them being lit up line by line, until the lighting party reached the last line.

'Come on then, lads, gi' us a leet or we'll never even see t'Charter,' said Eric Naylor, who was now alongside Ruth and Joshua, holding up his torch. As it took light and flared, Joshua could see that he was surrounded by the boys of Davey's gang who formed one of the lighting parties. Turning to his left, he could see that it was Jack lighting Ruth's torch.

'Glad to see me so soon?' asked Jack. 'Me and your Joshua'll 'ave another round soon, but I 'aven't got time now.'

Furious, Joshua poked his torch in Jack's direction, but his rival was already three lines away and hard at work. Jealous of Jack's important position, Joshua kept his silence. The Rochdale column halted and waited while all the torches were lit. Looking back, Ruth could see a forest of flares behind her; looking forward, the forest of Oldham flares was already moving away.

'Eh, Marion, I've never seen owt like this,' said Ruth as she turned her head from front to back, making semicircles in the air with her torch.

'And neither 'as anyone 'ere, lass,' said Marion.

'Torchlight marches are summut new. Supposed to put the fear o'God into t'government – Lord Melbourne and 'is men.'

Ralph Murphy, with the sinister face and twisted walking stick, who had never wanted women and children on the march, was standing not far behind. Ralph had said little throughout the march so far, but at the name of Lord Melbourne, the Prime Minister, his ears pricked up.

'An' do you think we'll frighten 'im, Marion?' he asked, in a surprisingly innocent tone.

'I don't see why not. Rich folk fear a fire more than owt.'

'You mean you'd gladly burn a few 'ouses down?'

'Did I say that, Ralph?'

'No, I were just wondering like.'

'Well, they'll not frighten General Napier whose just been made General in charge o'these parts,' said Jethro Strongitharm, resting on his crutch.

'An' what would frighten 'im, Jethro?' said Ralph.

'A crowd of marchers made up of Irish like you, I shouldn't wonder,' replied Jethro.

Ralph knew very well that Feargus O'Connor had been born in Ireland, but kept his counsel. Before tempers could rise higher, Jess Midgeley, seeing that the torches were lit right down the Rochdale column, gave the word to start moving.

As the haze of dusk turned into the blackness of night, the columns moved off one after the other. The torches of Ruth and Joshua were now burning brightly. Together with the thousand other torches in their column, they cast an eerie glow on the stonework of the houses. The children were amazed at the height of the mill buildings which they passed every quarter of a mile. They'd never seen buildings so tall. Sometimes there were mills on both sides, forming a canyon through which the columns passed.

As they moved down Ancoats Road and into Market Street, they could hear the Oldham column take up the refrain of the Chartist hymn '*Britannia's Sons, Though Slaves Ye Be*'. Recognising a tune they had learned at Sunday School the children listened to Marion's voice soaring above all those around her:

> "*All men are equal in His sight,*
> *The bond, the free, the black, the white!*
> *He made them all, – them freedom gave,*
> *He made the man, man made the slave!*"

The tall buildings on both sides made the singing echo from side to side so that the voices of a thousand marchers seemed more like those of five thousand.

The army officers were evidently disturbed by the force and power of the march and had stationed their cavalry at each of the streets leading off Oldham Road and Market Street. As the column marched down this road, Joshua could see the cavalry fingering their bridles and the horses pawing the ground. But the marchers showed no sign of breaking into a rabble, and the soldiers were under orders only to move if the march became a riot. Peterloo was strong in their minds too.

The march turned off Market Street to go the half-mile to St Peter's Field. Now the Rochdale marchers were going more slowly as the Oldham column fanned out into the square. Ruth and Joshua were glad enough to slow down, although the singing had prevented them from thinking how tired they were. Their column moved forward gradually until its turn came to enter St Peter's Field, when they were signalled to move into a different formation – in a long row four deep rather than a column – and lined up behind the Oldham marchers. As a result, Ruth, Joshua and Marion were at one end of the front row of their group and facing towards a raised platform which had been built of wood at one end of the Field.

As the other columns entered the Field and took up their places in rows, more and more of Manchester's citizens, many of whom had watched the march pass by, came to fill up every corner of space, nearly doubling the number of those who had been on the march to forty thousand. Nearly half of these had torches, augmenting the light from the rows of gas lamps which normally lit the edge of the Field.

As the marchers assembled in front of the platform, they found themselves beset by a small army of hawkers expecting to sell bread, biscuits, sweets, drinks – and copies of the Chartists' own *Northern Star* newspaper. There were few of the exhausted marchers, however, who had a penny or even a halfpenny to spare. Those selling drinks held a metal cup in one hand and a can of lemonade in the other. If they sold a cupful, they stood by while the customer swallowed it, gave the cup a rough wipe with a cloth and moved down the line looking for more business.

Ruth was the first in her row to receive the attentions of a drinks hawker who was hardly older than her.

'Come on then. Tha' looks as if tha' could do wi' summut to drink. Just a farthing from your aunty 'ere,' he said, pointing to Marion.

'An' where dust ah think I'll get a farthing from?' said Marion. 'This lass and lad have walked all o' twenty mile today. You should be congratulating 'em and pouring that drink free o'charge.'

'Well, twenty mile's none so bad. I'll fill you 'alf a cup free o'charge.'

'And give t'other 'alf to me brother,' said Ruth.

The hawker looked dubious but realising how little he was going to earn that night, poured out a full cup.

'That's for both o'you then,' he said, 'an' I'll watch while you drink it.'

'You first, Joshua,' said Ruth, 'but leave some for Marion; we'd never 'ave got this far without 'er.'

The hawker watched the children down their cups and pass what was left to Marion. As she was drinking, she became aware that a smartly dressed, tall man in a green suit and a grey top hat was watching her. When she had finished the cup and passed it back to the hawker, the man came over and spoke to her in a rounded English accent of a kind she'd never heard before. None of the wealthy mill masters in Todmorden, certainly not John Fielden, spoke that way.

'Excuse me, miss. Did I see that hawker give you and the children a free drink? And did I see them give their cup to you?'

'Aye, you did n'all for we've been marching together all't day: we all need to drink and none of us 'as got any brass. An' who might you be anyway?' said Marion.

'My name's William Steele from the newspaper *The Times*. I've come from London to write about this great meeting and let the Londoners know what kind of marchers are going to descend on them. Rabble, mob, or army of saints.'

'*The Times*? Oh, aye, I've 'eard of that,' said Marion. 'But who reads it anyway?'

'Anybody who is anybody – certainly everybody

in Parliament. The paper has changed the opinions of members a good many times, I can tell you.

'I've just been talking to your leaders on the platform – O'Connor and Fielden. They're afraid General Napier has given orders to the army to clear St Peter's Field as soon as the meeting begins. These torchlight parades were banned by the Home Secretary, Lord John Russell, last week, as soon as they were tipped off this one was coming.'

'But who'd tell 'em?' said Ruth, alert to the danger.

'Why, Russell's got his spies everywhere,' said Steele. 'He might even have one in this very row.'

'Tha'll not find a spy 'ere,' said Jim Knotts indignantly, who'd been listening to the conversation. 'No one what's prepared to walk two 'undred miles is going to spy for t'government at same time.'

'Well, they have had them before, and they certainly have them now,' said Steele. 'But are you children looking forward to marching all the way to London?'

'Well, we've decided to do it,' said Ruth.

'An' I reckon we will,' finished Joshua.

'Well, I've been told to join your march the whole way for my newspaper – so I'll watch out for you. What do you call yourselves?'

As the children gave their names, he wrote them down in a pocketbook. 'I must get closer to the platform now, but you'll see me again,' he said, moving forward through the rows made by the Oldham column.

'Well, I've never seen anyone dressed like that before,' said Marion.

'An' I've never 'eard anyone talk like that,' said Ruth.

'And never want to again, I should 'ope,' said Jim Knotts.

'Well, tha' may not like 'im, Jim, but what 'e said about soldiers and clearing t'field could be true. Look yonder,' said Marion, pointing to a corner of the square.

'By God, tha's reet, Marion,' said Jim.

'I can't see, I can't see,' said Joshua, who was not tall enough to see over the rows of Oldham marchers directly in front of him.

'Well, look then, lad. Get on me shoulders,' said Jim, crouching down so that Joshua could climb onto his shoulders. Once up, Joshua could see that at one corner of the field a unit of fusiliers were putting a big cannon into position. Looking to the nearest side of the field, he could see several hundred horsemen with their sabres rattling and their horses pawing the ground.

'Look, Jethro,' he cried, 'there's one of them big cannons what shot your leg off.'

Jethro was already examining the cannon, and his fury knew no bounds.

''Ow can they do it, lad?' he cried. 'It'll be nowt but full-blooded murder if they fire that thing. I'd never 'ave believed it could come to this. But stand your ground, lads, and they'll be too scared to fire.'

As he finished speaking, O'Connor's strong voice rang out across the square.

'Lads, liberty's taken another knock today. Melbourne and Russell have outlawed torchlit marches and meetings. Colonel Braithwaite of the fusiliers over there has told me he has orders to fire that cannon unless we disperse.

'Now what we want is the Charter – not marches, nor meetings, nor torches for themselves. We've got half a million signatures now – they're over there,' he said, pointing to the enormous scroll which Ruth and Joshua had first seen their father sign in Todmorden.

'By the time we get to London, we should have half a million more, and then Parliament'll not be able to stop us. If we have blood spilt here today, it'll set us back another five years.'

Ruth and Joshua heard shouts of agreement and disagreement around them. Eric Naylor was inclined to laugh off the danger: 'Not afraid of a toy gun, Feargus, a'ye?' he cried.

Jim Knotts looked at Jethro's one leg and said to Marion, 'Maybe 'e's right. I want to leave 'ere with two legs.' Ralph Murphy kept his counsel watching for his comrades' reactions. Ruth looked at her father, coming down the line towards them, suddenly aware of the danger his children were in.

'Aye, O'Connor's reet enough. This is a time for caution. It's more important to get to London wi't

Charter than to make a stand 'ere.'

O'Connor realised that he would have to use all his powers of persuasion to get the enormous crowd to disperse. His voice boomed out again.

'Let's be brave, lads. We've got to have the Charter, but we've got to 'ave the strength to fight for it. Shot to pieces, now, we'll never recover. Now I want you to put your torches out line by line – Oldham first, then Rochdale, then Salford and then the rest of you.'

It was a test of his ability to control the crowd. A few of the torches in the front row of the Oldham marchers were quenched; more were waved bravely in the air. O'Connor leaned down to speak to his close allies, Francis Place, a leading London Chartist, and John Fielden on the platform. They seemed to point in the direction of Ruth and Joshua. O'Connor rose again to his full height, saying:

'There are children no more than twelve years old here today, lads. Do you want them shot down? Should they be legless or armless? Will they get to London wi'us that way?'

More of the Oldham torches were extinguished, but still a good half were held high. Looking back to the cannon to his right, and the cavalry down the side of the field, O'Connor was increasingly worried.

'Let's have all the children twelve and under up here,' he cried. 'You mothers and fathers, release your young ones to us.'

Ruth turned to her father. 'Should we go, Dad?' she cried.

'Do we 'ave to?' said Joshua.

'Tha'd best go, the both of you,' said Jess quickly. 'Marion, will tha' go wi'em?'

'Come on, children, quickly,' said Marion, sensing the danger of the moment.

She moved forward round the Oldham line with Ruth and Joshua, walking the fifty yards up to the platform. As they climbed the few steps, another group of children were hard on their heels. Looking round, Joshua found himself staring right into the eyes of Jack, with Davey and the rest of his gang right behind him.

'All right, our Joshua?' said Jack, smiling mischievously as he climbed the steps.

'You wait,' said Joshua.

'None o'that, lads. Now come and line up there,' Marion said, pointing to the small space in front of O'Connor.

Ruth was amazed how different the scene appeared from the platform. Looking out over the crowd, she could see the thousands of torches still burning, the grey figures of the marchers standing close under them, the line of soldiers down the side of the square. She could see that it would be easy for many lives to be lost before her eyes.

O'Connor rose to his height, which seemed more imposing to Ruth as she stood a few feet away from him.

'Will you risk these lives then?' he cried back to the crowd.

'Or do we want these young heroes to fight on for the Charter through thick and thin – not disabled but rising above themselves on behalf of their fellowmen and women?' Davey grinned at Ruth and Joshua, delighted to be given the status of a hero. 'No, I plead with you; put out the torches tonight, that the torch of freedom may burn more brightly tomorrow.'

Slowly the torches in the front row of the Oldham column were put out. As the turn of later rows came, there was the same hesitation and uncertainty, but finally each of the torches was extinguished. O'Connor knew that he had control of the crowd now.

'Lads, I thank you for your brave act. The fight for the Charter is as strong as ever. Your column leaders know where your people are to sleep tonight. Our supporters in Manchester have taken every Sunday School 'all that would have us, every school house, every mill warehouse where the masters are for us. But you've not got long for sleep. We want a hundred men from each column on the Stockport road at seven tomorrow morning. We'll leave for London at eight.'

'An' will YOU be there?' said Joshua, turning to Jack.

'Not I,' said Jack. 'I'll leave that to you 'eroes from th'ills.'

'An' where'll you sleep tonight?' said Davey.

'They'll sleep wi't rest o' Rochdale column, in Oxford Road Sunday School,' said Marion.

'You could sleep on me mam's floor,' said Davey, relenting of his theft, and impressed that Ruth and Joshua really intended to carry on.

'Where's yer 'ouse then?' said Ruth.

'By t'Lock 50 on t'Bridgewater Canal,' replied Davey.

'We'll think on it another time. I like canals,' replied Ruth.

'Oh, so it's floating on canals and not marching on roads that tha' really like,' said a voice in a familiar accent close by.

Looking up, Ruth saw a face that looked both severe and kind, which she somehow felt she'd seen before but couldn't remember where. Marion recognised John Fielden immediately, for she'd sometimes seen him at the Unitarian Sunday School in Todmorden.

'Why, Mr Fielden, this 'as been a right close thing,' she said, bobbing slightly.

Fielden thought he recognised her face but couldn't place it.

'Yes, and you and t'children are brave to be 'ere,' he said. 'Where 'ave I seen you before?'

'At the Quakers in Todmorden,' Marion replied.

'Oh, from Tod; well, that's grand. And will you march tomorrow?'

'Yes, Mr Fielden, we're going all the way to London and Parliament,' said Joshua.

'Well it's just as well, because it's me and my friend Thomas Attwood from Birmingham who'll be presenting t'Charter to Parliament. But after that, you'd better come and see me. My 'ouse is in Panton Street and I fancy you'll need feeding up by the time you've walked those two 'undred miles. See that they come,' he said to Marion, and left the platform with O'Connor as the massive crowd dispersed in all directions, leaving the cannon and the cavalry presiding over the Field.

CHAPTER 5

THE DERBYSHIRE HILLS

At seven o'clock the next morning, the marchers were assembling on the road that led out from Manchester to Stockport. As Ruth and Joshua, together with their father, Marion and the other Todmorden marchers approached the crowd, they could barely see through the cold mist of an autumn morning which had been turned into a thick fog by the smoke belching from hundreds of mill chimneys. Jim Knotts carried their banner furled round its two poles. The road they were walking down was packed with horse-drawn carts moving bales of cotton and woven cloth from one mill to another and down to the warehouses on the banks of the Ashton and Stockport Canals.

'I think I can see t'march gathering now at bottom of this road. They look more like ghosts than men,' said Joshua.

''Appen last night took flesh and blood off 'em,' joked Marion.

'Aye, an' this week may tak it off us too,' said Jim Knotts.

'Fancy arriving in London as a skeleton, Josh?'

It was only when they were twenty yards away from the gathering marchers that Ruth and Joshua could see that hundreds of their comrades from last night had responded to O'Connor's call and were ready to set off for the south and London. But in the cold, damp air, as they waited for the march to begin, they drew blankets round their shoulders or huddled over small fires – many made from the sticks of the torches quenched in the previous night's meeting. Ruth wondered how this dishevelled crowd would ever regain yesterday's strength.

As they moved closer to one group huddled round a fire, Jess Midgeley was accosted by Frank Sykes, the organiser of the Oldham marchers:

'Now, Jess, come on; we've got to get these lads organised. Same order of march as yesterday, so that puts you behind us. I reckon we've got about one 'undred lads from each of yesterday's columns – so about two thousand all told. Can you get your lot up to t'front then?'

'Where would that be?' said Jess. 'I can't see nowt for this fog.'

'About three 'undred yards down t'road. O'Connor's already there an' 'e wants to discuss t'route wi'you. There's a new idea come up. Tha'd best get down there.'

'Come on, children. Let's get down t'road to t'front,' said Marion, holding their hands.

As they walked through the crowd of marchers, Ruth noticed that there were hardly any women, and no children. Her heart fell as she realised they would have only adults with them in this ordeal. Marion was a kind of friend, but she was, after all, also an adult. She might pass on whatever Ruth and Joshua said to their father. The other Todmorden marchers were a strange group: she liked Eric Naylor and Jim Knotts, was a bit scared of Judd with his hammer and Jethro with his crutch, and found Ralph Murphy, with his twisted walking stick and habit of asking questions, to be quite sinister. They were not the companions she would have chosen for a two hundred-mile walk, but at least her dad and Marion were with them.

Moving down the road, they eventually saw the Oldham banner and about fifty of the Oldham contingent lining up behind it. O'Connor and Place were standing close by it, deep in conversation with the tall man in a grey top hat whom Marion recognised from the night before as the journalist William Steele. The bugler was standing close by them. Seeing them coming, and recognising Ruth and Joshua from the previous night, O'Connor broke off the discussion and stepped forward: 'Now, here come the most valuable marchers of all. Having them with us is worth a thousand signatures on the Charter. Don't you agree, Mr Steele?'

'Why yes, I do. And how are you today, Ruth and Joshua?'

'Oh, not so bad,' said Joshua. 'We 'ad a good sleep at t'Sunday School and they fed us wi' some right nice porridge for us breakfast.'

'Ready for a trip into the hills?'

'Anytime,' said Joshua. 'That's where we come from, y'know.'

But at this, Jess Midgeley and the other Todmorden marchers looked worried. They had been ready to go through the textile towns south of Manchester, from Stockport to Buxton, but going over the moors was a very different matter. None of them knew the Derbyshire hills that lay to the south-east, but as men of the Pennines, they realised the dangers of an upland route.

Seeing their uncertainty, O'Connor stepped in: 'Lads, last night showed us how far the government's prepared to go. If we give them a chance they'll spill blood, and we don't want a violent fight. General Napier has sent a message to say he'll be ready to break up any march through Derbyshire. As many of our committee as could meet last night have decided we should split into two parties – one to go over the moors and the other to go through the towns to Buxton, and march on to Nottingham, where there's plenty of support. We'll 'ave most of the city with us there and should be safe enough.

'But with two parties marching in the same direction by different routes, the army will be confused, and the cavalry won't like it with peat bogs and cliffs. So we reckon Charter and Petition'll be safer with the moorland group. Will you be on it?'

Jess spoke for the Todmorden group.

'Mr O'Connor, we don't know them Derbyshire 'ills, but we know the moors round our way, and we know they can be treacherous. There'll be peat bogs up there, and 'illsides wi' loose rocks and stones, and a few cliffs, I shouldn't wonder. Wi t'mists you get this time o'year owt could 'appen. Just 'ow many men do you want to go that way?'

'Well, we reckon we should keep the biggest number in the towns to distract army and the police – so we want about five 'undred to go over the top. We'd like to keep marchers from your part of Lancashire together – with the lads from Oldham, Rochdale, Burnley and that area, we'll 'ave a good strong crowd that should be able to stand up to whatever comes.'

Here, he dropped his voice and looked straight at Jess. He had the air of someone used to persuading people to do something they didn't really wish to do.

'Mr Midgeley, I reckon your children'll be safer on the top. I fear we may have terrible trouble in the towns.'

Jess paused and thought a little. He realised O'Connor could be right; and besides, his children were used to the moors. He turned to discuss it with the other members of the Todmorden group, who were not likely to be persuaded by arguments about what was best for the Midgeley children. Judd, with his hammer still over his shoulder, was as usual ready for anything; Ralph looked impassive as if waiting to see which way the others would jump; Jim, ever ready for an adventure, looked happy at the prospect; Jethro, usually anxious to show that his one leg was no handicap, looked doubtful. 'Peat bogs and this one leg'll 'appen not go together,' he said to Jess.

Marion despaired at the thought of Ruth and Joshua struggling over the moors in weather which might rapidly get worse, but she could see it might be the safer course. Not wishing to give away her feelings, she looked at Ruth and Joshua.

'Well, you two,' she said, 'what'll it be then: more grimy towns or God's open moorland?'

In turn, Ruth and Joshua looked at each other: they loved the moors but knew their dangers too. For Joshua, moors meant not only space and freedom from the cramped life of the mill, but also the memory of having his ankle bitten by the farmers' dogs on Langfield Common. He wondered if gamekeepers patrolled the route into Derbyshire. But gathering his courage and looking at Ruth, he replied: 'Let's go by t'moors. I've 'ad enough o' towns.'

Ruth could see the dangers even more clearly, as she felt her coat with its odd shape made by her mother from her one blanket. But she sensed that her father had been persuaded by O'Connor's arguments that the moorland route would be safer for his children, and decided not to complicate the question.

'Aye, a'm with you, Josh. Let's get on wi't, Marion.'

'Well, Jess, you've got two troopers 'ere,' said Marion.

Jess Midgeley was not given the chance to take the discussion further, as O'Connor intervened:

'Congratulations, Mr Midgeley. You've got a courageous group from Todmorden. We'll count on you to be in the forefront of the moorland marchers.' He moved down the line without giving Jess a chance to reply.

O'Connor had an uncanny ability to look people straight in the eye and gauge how much they could be persuaded to do for him and the Chartist movement. By a combination of bluster, patience and determination, he had already mobilised the most effective peaceful protest movement Britain had ever seen. So far, there had been no major setbacks, and his confidence in his ability to get his way was overwhelming. Ruth had been shocked that he'd not given her father the chance to reply on behalf of the Todmorden group. As she now watched him move down the line, she could see him spend a few minutes with selected leaders, and guessed that he was imposing his will on them just as he had done on her group.

Within half an hour, he was back level with Ruth and Joshua, pausing only to say to their father:

'That's settled. The first five 'undred'll go over the top with you. All the rest are going on by Stockport and Buxton – I'll stick with them, but we want the Charter and Petition carried over the top to keep it well clear of the army. There's nothing they'd like better than to see thousands of Chartists arriving in London with no Charter, no Petition and no signatures. The Oldham lads will carry the Petition but I'd like your group to carry the Charter.'

He moved on without waiting for an answer, as Ruth observed the look of concern and worry on her father's face. He was going to find this a new and heavy burden.

One thing was clear to Jess: Jethro Strongitharm with his one leg and crutches could not march with them over the hills. He would have to stay with the group whose route lay through the towns and valleys. The old soldier did not take much persuading, but Jess wanted to make sure he was well looked after, and knew that Joshua in particular would be sorry to lose his company.

'Joshua, you and I'll go together wi' Jethro back to t'Stockport group and see 'e's alreet wi 'them.'

Joshua needed no prompting and Jethro was glad enough to have the support. The leader of the Stockport marchers, Ben Mather, was a young, fairly well-dressed man in his thirties who Jess Midgeley recognised as having been on the platform of speakers on the previous evening in Manchester.

'Aye, that's right enough,' he said, when Jess mentioned the plan. 'The executive committee what met last night reckoned it'd be best way to make sure at least a few 'undred of us get to London. Feargus was dead right on that, and t'members didn't tak much persuading.'

'Well, we're prepared to follow t'Oldham group over t'moor, but Jethro 'ere, who's already lost a leg for England, shouldn't be facing them peat bogs, an' we thought 'appen he could march with you.'

'Aye, and spy out the soldiers for you,' said Jethro, leaning on his crutch. 'Now that the Duke's turned on 'is own men, you need a few that's seen military tactics.'

'You're welcome to march with us,' said Ben Mather. 'Just stay close to me.'

'Well, Jess,' said Jethro, 'this is more than a day out, and I wonder when we'll get them Parliament men in our sights. Young Joshua, I'm right sorry to part wi'you. I'll miss you, lad, look after thissen.' He stretched his hand out and Joshua took it, turning away hurriedly.

Father and son walked back to the Todmorden group, each more gloomy for the loss of Jethro.

The Oldham marchers were now impatient to be off. Behind them, the columns of the five towns selected for the moorland journey were also in line and ready to leave.

The petition with its half-million signatures was now rolled up and carried by three of the Oldham marchers, one behind the other.

They were going to march east of Manchester through Denton and Hyde to Glossop, and then on to the top of the Pennines and southwards to Matlock and Nottingham. A break in the column followed the Rochdale marchers: all those behind it were going to take the lowland route through Stockport, and then south-east to Matlock and Nottingham. The two columns would regroup in Matlock and march as one into Nottingham, where support for the Charter was strong.

O'Connor and Place were standing at the front of the Oldham column, ready to give the signal to move. There was a bugler by their side: a veteran of peacetime service with the Lancashire Fusiliers who had now thrown in his lot with the Chartists.

'Now come on, Tommy, let's have a blast on that bugle and get them on their way,' said O'Connor.

From their position behind the Oldham marchers, Ruth and Joshua could clearly hear the reveille sounded on the bugle, and felt ready for a long day's march. Joshua imagined himself marching off to Waterloo with Jethro; Ruth wondered if the clouds would clear and they could sleep under an open sky full of stars. Both drew comfort from the fact that Marion was beside them, apparently as cheerful as ever. While waiting for the sign to move, Marion and Jim Knotts had started joking to keep themselves alert:

'Well, Jim, finally in the real world, lad, aren't thou? – beats cracking jokes in Tod Market.'

'This the real world? Tha' mun be joking, Marion. Real world begins in Derbyshire where ah grew up, and where we're 'eading now. I'll soon show tha' the gates of Paradise.'

'Oh, so you and the angels were kissing cousins, were tha'?' said Marion. 'I almost wish I'd been there.'

'Tha' wouldn't 'a wished to be wi' me in the kind of nursery I were in,' said Jim, turning serious.

'An' what were that?' said Marion, catching his mood.

'Why, my nursery were Arkwright's mill at Cressbrook, where he kept over two 'undred orphans from London,' said Jim, adding shyly, 'an' I were one on'em.'

'Well, who'd a thought it, young Jim. Wi' you talking proper Lancashire like.'

'A' can as soon talk Lunnon as Lancashire,' said Jim. 'Not to mention Derbyshire, by the way,' and he launched into the national anthem cockney style:

God sive our groycious queen,
Long live our noble queen,
God sive the queen.

'Ooh, sounds awful,' chipped in Ruth. 'Just as well tha' learned to speak rightly.'

'Well, that's just 'cause I escaped from Arkwright's place and came to Lancashire,' said Jim.

'Escaped?' said Joshua. ''Ow dust'a do that?'

'There's a river what runs by Cressbrook Mill, and mill t' depends on three water wheels in t'river. Top one is small enough, 'appen four feet across, but it gets stuck easy wi' driftwood and that. They used to send me and one other lad down to tak out driftwood, an' one day we were told to go when it were right dark in winter – after five o'clock in th'evening. As we walked down t'river to t' wheel, we both looked at each other and knew what were on us minds. We never stopped at the wheel but ran on and on down the river path, through woods and steep valleys, some with great cliffs rising as far as you could make out.

'Every now and then, t'path 'ud leave river and go through a village or line of 'ouses, and sometimes another mill. After more miles than I'd like to count, we were running through another mill yard by the river, and Jamie – that were me friend – slipped an' fell. A great big man, what looked like an overseer, came out and put his boot on 'im, saying, "No, you don't, ya young puppy. I can see tha's from Mr Arkwright's mill down yonder."

"'Let me go, let me go," said Jamie. But there was no way that brute were going to release 'im.

"'Run for it, Jim," cried Jamie as the overseer pulled 'im up by scruff of 'is neck. And that I did, faster 'n before, though I thought I were already puffed out. Tho' t'overseer shouted at me too, I got through yard and back t'river path outside the glow of t'mill's oil lamps.'

'What then?' said Joshua, alive with interest.

'Well, there were nowt for it but to carry on till I dropped exhausted and slept in bushes by river. It were ducks what waked me up in't morning, and I walked on as far as I could. After a while, path came to pike road an' I'd no choice but to follow it through t'ills to Buxton. There weren't much traffic on that road, an' tho' I got a few stares, no one took much notice of me.

'When a'got to Buxton I found my way t'market where I met some lads, and there were two brothers amongst them what were right friendly. They took me 'ome an' their family adopted me. I were twelve then, and a good winder. It weren't long afore I could find work in a spinning mill and soon began to pay me way.'

'So 'ow did tha' get to Tod then?' said Joshua, swept up in Jim's story.

'Well, after a couple of years I reckoned they'd 'ad enough o' me, and I said me thanks and farewells and pushed on to Manchester which were too big. I needed a small town where I could make friends more easy like, and so I came on t'canal one day to your place, worse luck,' he finished with a smile.

Marion was taken aback by Jim's powers of survival. The sandy-haired joker she had always regarded as something of a layabout must have plenty of courage and determination. Ruth and Joshua were amazed at how much Jim had done alone when he was about their age.

The bugle reveille had alerted the whole line of marchers to action. The Oldham column set out on the road for Denton and Glossop, with the Todmorden group falling in behind, followed by the columns from the other three towns. As they filed past O'Connor, he gave them a cheerful wave, pleased to see that the argument he had put to Jess Midgeley had prevailed. They noticed William Steele standing close behind him and were delighted to see him raise his top hat in salute to them.

Their spirits were not depressed by the long march through Denton to the east. They soon left the industrial heart of Manchester: the cannons of mills and warehouses of the kind they had passed through the previous day fell away within a mile to the green fields of Openshaw. Soon they were in an area of hamlets and farmsteads scattered between fields, still a faded gold after haymaking. Looking beyond the fields, they could see the shape of the familiar moors not more than ten miles away.

At first, it had seemed to Ruth and Joshua that it would not take more than half a morning to get to the bottom of the moors, and then the whole column would be up and away, marching easily up to and along the top. But in fact it took more than five hours for the column to reach the end of the walled fields and the beginning of the rough moorland. The people of the farmsteads through which they passed had, for the most part, looked at them with disapproval. Although many of them had members of their family who worked in the mills in Manchester, their main livelihood was from the sale of meat, eggs and oatcakes in the city. Anything which savoured of a strike could mean a loss of income, and they were likely to be against it.

Ruth was surprised to notice one big old man with a crook and a sheepdog who had watched them from in front of a stone wall, shaking his head. She just caught him saying, apparently to his dog:

'T'city of Jericho u'd never fall to a crowd o' this ilk, now would it, Lassie?'

She couldn't help giving the farmer a smile as she walked past, but as she walked on, just caught him saying:

'An' wilt 'a still smile on top o'Kinder Scout, lass?' She began to wonder if she would.

As the column approached the end of the lane between the fields, Frank Sykes and Jess Midgeley had walked together to agree on how best to organise the march over the top. They both knew that Matlock lay about fifty miles to the south-east, but neither had covered the ground by the high or the low route. Jess had heard that Jim Knotts had come from close to Matlock and asked him how much he knew. Jim had told him that he would be able to help once they got over into Miller's Dale where Cressbrook Mill was, but that he had never been over Kinder Scout, whose mass now loomed before them. Frank and Jess concluded that they at least needed directions from someone who knew the moor, and afterwards accosted one of the farmers as they marched through his yard.

'Begging tha' pardon, which way should we be going to top o' Kinder Scout to get down into Derbyshire?'

'Tha' mun be careful, lads, tha' might lose a few to 'peat and cliffs an' there could be a storm brewing up today. Best way is yon track as they call Doctor's Gait and then to turn south through peat bogs on't top. But there's nobbut sheep tracks up there to show t'way. Now I could give thee my lad Enoch?'

Frank and Jess were quick to seize the opportunity. 'Well, that'd be grand. For we mun get to Matlock in three days. We've not time to get lost.'

At this, the farmer turned to a dark-haired boy of about twelve standing close to him.

'Enoch, lad, wilt'a go over't top wi'em? Up t'gait an' over t'rocks. 'Think on at Devil's Rock, though, lad. Tha' never knows what tha'll find there.'

Enoch nodded. He'd already decided he preferred sheep to people, but he also liked the moor better than anywhere and knew it like the back of his hand. He was happy to show his knowledge to this crowd of strangers, provided that he wasn't expected to speak to them. Ruth and Joshua, not far away, were glad to see that there was now at least one person of their own age on the march.

Few of the marchers were used to rough walking, and fewer still had boots which would turn the water in the peat bogs. A good half were wearing clogs with wooden soles which were comfortable enough on the flat surfaces of streets and mill floors, but were too loose to provide support on rough moorland. Others had old leather shoes which, even if waterproof, failed to cover their ankles. Most were wearing rough woollen jackets which provided little enough protection for the walk to work on a cold autumn morning, and would provide even less for the walk over the top. They had been marching three abreast on the ground they had covered so far. As they began to climb up the moorland track, the marchers adopted their own pace, and the lines of three abreast were replaced by straggling columns of individuals.

Ruth and Joshua, much more used to the moor than most of the marchers, soon found themselves moving further and further ahead along the column. Marion struggled to keep up with them, and finding herself out of breath, would drop back as soon as she drew level with them. Before long, the two children drew level with their father; Frank Sykes and the farmer's son, Enoch.

'No straggling fro' you two then,' said Jess, giving them a quick smile. 'Where's Marion? Tha's not left 'er behind, 'ave thee?'

'Oh, she's back yonder wi' Jim Knotts,' said Ruth, turning round and pointing down the moor. Jess turned round looking for Marion and Jim and was disturbed to see how spread out the line had become.

'They're straggling too much, Frank,' he said. 'We may start losing 'em.'

'Aye, and stragglers'll not find them farming folk too 'elpful,' said Frank Sykes quietly, so that the boy Enoch would not hear. 'Tha'd best go down t'line, Jess, and keep behind them as is falling back. Tha' childer can stay wi'me.'

'Well, I'll fall back a bit, but I'm not playing nursemaid to every straggler from Bolton and Burnley, or we'll never get t'Charter to London. Tha'd best stay at front now wi' Frank, you two,' he said to Ruth and Joshua, while standing aside to let the line pass him.

Ruth and Joshua needed little encouragement to keep at the front of the marchers. They found that the pace set by Frank Sykes was easy for them, and they liked keeping in step with Enoch, who led them confidently up a moorland track. The route had been developed to take rock from a quarry towards the top of the moor, but the quarry had become exhausted as a result of the never-ending demand for stone to build mills and houses in Manchester. The track was now overgrown and small bogs were forming along it. Enoch seemed to know where these were before coming to them, and frequently jumped over them. Ruth and Joshua did not see them so clearly and found water seeping over the top of their clogs before they had time to pull their feet out.

Ruth found herself turning round every five minutes to see how far Marion had dropped back. She could still make her out about halfway down the winding and ragged line of marchers. Joshua looked back even more often to see whether he could still see his father. He was not sure whether the hazy figure who seemed to interrupt his walk every few minutes to talk to stragglers was him or not. But he could see that most of those who seemed to be turning back were persuaded to change their mind and rejoin the column.

As Joshua pulled his left clog out of another small bog, he was reminded of the attack from the dogs on the Todmorden moors three years ago. The hounds which had been set on him had been patrolling a very similar stretch of moorland.

'D'tha' 'ave keepers up 'ere then?' he said to Enoch,

who up to that moment had led the column in total silence.

It was the one topic on which Enoch was willing to speak immediately.

'Keepers? Aye, we do an'all. An' they can make us life murder. If there's one sheep that strays off common land onto Duke o' Devonshire's moor, we'll never see 'im again. An' if we chase 'em onto t'Duke's moor, there's a 'ole pack of 'ounds as'll tear us flesh off if we're not careful.'

'An' 'ow much land does the Duke 'ave then?' asked Joshua.

'From top o t'moor yonder down t'other side to Chatsworth House, that's 'appen thirty mile, though neither me dad nor any other sheep owners 'ave been near there.'

'An' 'ow much land do you 'ave?'

'All tha' can see to t'top yonder and over to just below Kinder Scout top. They say it's about a thousand acres, but there's more than twenty farmers what are grazing it and not enough grass for any of 'em. It's only six months since Jimmy Walton lost 'is two rams to t'Duke's men.'

Ruth could see that the silent Enoch had something to say after all.

'When'll we get to t'top then?' she asked.

''Appen another hour, if you don't slow down,' said Enoch. 'An' then we've got to turn along 'top and through them deep peat bogs to get onto Kinder Scout.'

'What's Kinder Scout?' said Joshua.

'Tha' don't know Kinder Scout?' said Enoch in an unbelieving tone. 'It's the 'ighest peak for miles. That great black mass tha' could see as tha' walked from Manchester.'

Joshua remembered the dark, high hill the marchers could see on the horizon as they left the streets of Manchester. As they had drawn nearer to the lower hills, they had lost sight of it beyond the horizon, but Joshua remembered it well enough to see it would be no easy walk for the straggling column of five hundred marchers.

''Ow soon will we be there then?' asked Ruth.

'Well, me and me dog Shep 'ud tak about an 'our to top, 'appen two hours from 'ere. But wi'you lot, it'll tak 'appen three. An' if I'm going to show thee way into Edale, that's way we'll be going.'

The track was now sloping steeply upwards, which even in completely dry conditions would have been a hard pull. With water seeping back into the ground after recent rainfall, with poor footwear, and after the previous day's events, there were many on the march whose hearts began to weaken as they saw the climb that still lay before them. Frank Sykes could not help a look of dismay pass across his face as he looked back down the column to see the gap between marchers widening. He hoped that Jess Midgeley would be able to persuade those at the back not to turn round and walk back into Manchester.

As Ruth, Joshua and Enoch approached Kinder Scout at the head of the column, the peak passed out of view again and they found themselves at the bottom of a steep slope of scree and boulders, stretching hundreds of feet above them.

'Fancy a run up there?' said Enoch, leaping ahead with his dog Shep.

Not willing to be outdone, and keen to show that they could manage any moorland track, Ruth and Joshua scrambled ahead of the column with Enoch. Moving quickly from boulder to boulder, they had climbed halfway up to the top before turning round to see the marchers spread out into a line that was longer than ever. About a hundred feet below them, Frank Sykes, still the first of the adults, looked with increasing dismay at the state of his followers. It was now mid-afternoon and the sky was darkening as the storm which Enoch's father had predicted seemed to be coming closer. He could hardly see the end of the column as it stretched so far back, or make out Jess Midgeley who was supposed to be keeping the marchers together. About five hundred yards away, not yet on the scree, he recognised Marion walking with Jim Knotts in a group of about twenty, but well separated from those in front and behind. Two of their group were carrying the Charter rolled up and strung on a pole between them. Looking up, he saw the three children getting too far ahead – so much so that Enoch's knowledge of the path might be lost to them.

'Hey, you three, slow down,' he called up the scree. But as he looked up, he could see a flash of lightning illuminate the sky. It came again and, looking down, he could see the whole column lit up against the moor. As the lightning flashed, the three children jumped under the nearest boulder and crouched there as the bright fork flashed above Kinder Scout.

'A've never seen owt like this,' said Enoch. 'It's like th'end of t'world.'

'God should be on our side, not sending us to 'ell,' said Ruth.

'Well, 'appen it'll keep redcoats off t'moor,' said Joshua, 'an' give us a fair run over't top.'

As he spoke, a great clap of thunder seemed to burst above them and they crawled further under the overhang of the boulder. They heard the first hiss of the rain as it struck the moor about a mile away, and then saw it driving down into the column of marchers as they struggled towards the scree. They watched as some marchers huddled together and then turned round and moved in the opposite direction. They thought they could make out Marion and Jim waving their hands and urging those closest to them to make for the rock and use its shelter. Suddenly they could see Jess Midgeley running towards them. Struggling up the hill, he caught up first with Frank Sykes.

'This is bad,' he said. 'We'll never keep 'em together in this. 'Alf of those at back 'ave already turned round.

They've no stomach for Kinder Scout in a storm o'this kind. Where's Ruth and Joshua then?'

'Up front under them boulders wi' young Enoch.'

'I'm going to them. You do what you can to get rest up to these rocks.'

Joining the children, Jess crouched down with them. 'All right, you three?' he managed to ask cheerfully enough.

'As well as may be in the middle of a storm wi' only me old blanket for a coat,' said Ruth. 'Mam would love to see how well we're doing.'

Jess smiled wryly and wondered briefly if his wife Ellen was even now looking out on the storm as it hit their cottage in Todmorden. But his mind quickly returned to the need to get the marchers across the moor as soon as possible.

''Ow far from 'ere, Enoch lad?' he said.

'A good three hours down into Edale, but there's plenty of shelter when tha' gets there.'

'An' over top: 'ow hard will it be?'

'Well, there's a good sheep track, and I can find t'way alreet. But there's a big drop down t'cliff face on t'south, just about where the stream comes out they call the Spout. An' then of course there's Jacob's Ladder.'

'Jacob's Ladder. What's that?' said Jess.

'It's a right steep path that goes down into Edale,' said Enoch. 'I've only been down it twice, but each time I fair rolled down.'

'An' what kind of shelter would we find there?' asked Jess.

'Well, there's me cousin Nelly what married a Derbyshire man called John Gaunt, and they've got a right big barn.'

'Which like as not will be full of 'ay now,' muttered Jess.

'So when this storm's over, or if it is, we should still be able to get there by nightfall?'

'Well, me an' Shep would. Whether yer 'ole lot will, I couldn't rightly say.'

Looking back down the scree, Jess could see that the line had divided into two clear groups – about two thirds who were reversing their steps, and a third who were moving upwards to the scree. He was relieved to see that the second group included Marion and Jim, and the marchers who were carrying the Charter. Frank Sykes had gone down to meet them, and the whole group was now struggling up the hill in the driving rain.

'Well, we'll wait for 'em 'ere and let 'em all shelter till storm's past,' said Jess to the children.

Ruth, Joshua and Enoch were now sodden from top to toe and scared stiff of the thunder which continued to roll around the sky, as the rain came down in sheets.

'Well,'appen me mam wouldn't be so pleased to see us 'ere now,' said Ruth, beginning to shiver as the rain reached her skin.

'Like as not, lass,' said Jess, beginning to wish he was home with Ellen himself.

Frank Sykes now struggled up the scree with the vanguard of the rest of the marchers; and within a few minutes, Marion and Jim were with them too.

'Christ Almighty, this is terrible,' said Marion as she reached the children, water dripping from her hair but a warm smile of relief on her face as she saw Ruth and Joshua with Enoch and Shep, huddled under the rock. 'Now, you nuisances; make way for me and Jim,' she cried, as the two of them took up what little remaining space lay under the boulder.

Ten minutes later, a crowd of about two hundred marchers – all that was left of the five hundred which had set off that morning – had gathered at the scree and were crouching behind the rocks and boulders which gave them very limited shelter against the rainstorm. The two men carrying the Charter had wrapped it in a heavy blanket to give it whatever protection it could provide against the storm.

Frank Sykes joined Jess Midgeley, crouching close to Ruth and Joshua. 'This is terrible, Jess,' he said. 'We've lost more than 'alf 'o t'marchers, and God knows if we can continue over t'top i'this state.'

'Enoch 'ere says we can get to Edale where there's

shelter like as not in about three hours if we keep going.'

'Aye, if's the word,' said Frank. 'O'Connor never reckoned on this. Marchers on t'other route'll be clear of this like as not, sheltering in some chapel or Sunday School.'

''Appen we should be joining 'em,' said Jess doubtfully. 'That way, we'd stand a chance of keeping more of our men together.'

Ruth looked at her father in disbelief. She was suddenly afraid that he was contemplating turning round because he was afraid for Joshua and herself. She wouldn't hear of that.

'Nay, Dad, we've come this far now. Tha'd not wish us back off t'moor?'

'Well, no lass, tha's reet enough.'

As they spoke, Enoch was pointing out to Joshua a brighter patch of sky on the horizon, where it looked as if it had stopped raining.

'Dad,' said Joshua, 'Look over yonder. 'Appen we'll all be out o't rain afore long.'

'Aye, Dad,' said Ruth, anxious to press her point. 'We've got to keep going now.'

Even Enoch was concerned that he might not be able to show his skills in navigating the march over the most difficult and dangerous part of Kinder Scout.

'It'll be worse for 'em what turned back,' he said with a face full of gloom. 'When it rains, them peat bogs'll drag you down, and there's more than one shepherd's boy been lost that way.'

Jess and Frank looked nervously back towards the peat bogs they'd crossed a few hours ago. They could already see, through the rain, a group of marchers struggling through the peat and going ever more slowly. Some were up to their knees in peat, and seemed to be sinking further. Jess and Frank needed no further encouragement to press ahead rather than retreat. They could see that turning back would not lead to regrouping but to a rout. As soon as the bright patch in the sky spread more widely and the rain lightened, they would press ahead up the scree and over the top.

Enoch held Shep close to him. The dog had been badly frightened by the thunder and lightning and began to whimper in his master's arms. But as the storm subsided, his ears pricked up and, looking up the scree, he could see a flock of a dozen sheep huddled a hundred yards away. He pushed against Enoch's arms, anxious to be away now; but Enoch held him back, whispering into his ears, 'Not yet, lad, not yet.'

In another ten minutes the rain had almost stopped; and Frank, standing to his full six feet, shook the rain from his woollen coat and raising his right hand waved to the whole group to carry on with the climb up the scree. Looking down at Enoch, still under the rock, he said, 'Right, lad; let's get on wi'it then. Can'st 'a get us into Edale before night?'

'Aye, and to a right good fire to dry us selves on?' said Joshua.

Enoch, reverting to his silent self, spoke only to Shep.

'Right, boy; you're away now.'

No sooner had he spoke than Shep dashed up the scree and made for the flock of sheep at the top. Enoch watched him go but gave a piercing whistle as he reached the flock. Shep stopped in mid-dash and crouched down again, awaiting his master's orders. Another shorter piercing whistle followed quickly from Enoch's pursed lips.

'He'll sit still there now,' said Enoch to Frank and Jess. 'Tha'd best get lads and,' as he looked doubtfully at Ruth and Marion, 'lasses up to 'im.'

The marchers staggered up the scree, shaking water from their rough coats and grasping boulders to give them a hold. Enoch, Ruth and Joshua were up at the front and were the first to arrive where Shep still lay crouching. Looking down, they could see that all those who were still with them were onto the scree. Enoch, impressed by the need now to get into Edale before nightfall, gave another whistle; and he and Shep dashed ahead along a path which Ruth and Joshua could only just make out.

The path lay along the southern edge of Kinder Scout and, as the clouds cleared, the children could see far down over a series of cliffs into a wooded valley below.

'An' 'ow far's that to t'bottom?' asked Ruth as she looked down.

'Me dad says tha' could 'appen fall 'alf a mile and never a stop' said Enoch.

Joshua, casting another glance over the cliffs, fell behind Ruth into single file.

The rest of the marchers were now reaching the top of the scree. None of the Todmorden group had turned back, and they had stayed within range of each other. Eric Naylor, still with a grin on his face, and Judd Ackroyd, using his great hammer to support him through the scree, arrived at the top together. Ralph Murphy was about fifty yards behind them, but proved surprisingly agile, barely using his twisted walking stick. The two Oldham marchers carrying the Charter were not far from him, and Frank Sykes and Jess were still at the top of the scree, directing marchers down the path which Marion and Jim had already followed, just making out the figures of the children and Shep as they led the way along the path.

As he came to the top of the scree, Ralph Murphy came up to Frank and Jess and pointed back to the peat bogs where those who had turned back could be seen staggering through the morass.

'So what made tha' send 'em back then? Can't you see how they're struggling?' he said.

'Sent 'em back!' said Frank. 'We've no more sent 'em back than that damned Napier sent us 'ere. They couldn't face moors i' this storm and that's all there is to it.'

'Ah, so it'll not be on your 'ead then,' said Ralph, almost to himself, joining the other marchers as they moved forward.

Enoch and Shep led the way along the path that continued to follow the side of the cliff. Sometimes it was just above the rocks, sometimes it led through the rocks in the upper part of the cliff. To their left, the great mass of the peak of Kinder Scout continued to be surrounded by swirling mist. To their right, they looked down from an enormous height into the wooded valleys which lay to the south. But the path was narrow and, in many parts, difficult to see, and even Enoch had to watch it carefully to make sure that he did not stumble. Ruth and Joshua were nimble enough in following his footsteps but realised that a false step could easily give them a sprained ankle or a broken leg. Many of the older marchers, townsfolk for all or most of their lives, were clearly terrified and moved so slowly that the foremost only just kept the three children and Shep in view.

After leading the way along the path for about half an hour, the children came to an area of barren rocks where the moor edge turned a corner and ran southwards. The rocks appeared to be about a hundred yards across; but as they walked over them, they could see a rushing torrent running through the centre, sweeping towards the cliff face. The stream was about four feet across and with no sign of rocks to act as stepping stones.

''Ow do we get across this then, Enoch?' said Ruth.

''A've never seen it this 'igh,' said Enoch. 'It's what they call Kinder Downfall, and it's generally nobbut a beck, 'appen 'alf as wide as this. Tha' can span it in a stride.'

'An' where would tha' cross when it's low ?' asked Joshua.

'Somewhere there, by yon big rock. But I'd best try it wi' me stick first.'

Enoch went forward with the other two to the side of the stream and gingerly poked into the water with his stick to find its depth. It went down about two feet and seemed to find the bottom.

'Well, that's not bad,' said Enoch. 'We can tak a risk wi' that.'

'What about Shep?' said Ruth, looking concerned as the dog stood with his ears pricked upwards, now barking at the flood.

'We'll be all right, boy, won't we?' said Enoch, picking up Shep in his arms and putting his right foot carefully into the water. In spite of his rough clothes, Enoch had a good pair of farm boots on, and they found the bottom of the clough easily, though the water was up above his knees. Wading through, with Shep in his arms, he was over safely enough.

'Now then,' he said, 'let's 'ave you two safely over, and then we can worry about t'rest,' who were now appearing at the beginning of the expanse of rocks which stretched away from the stream bed. Marion and Jim were at the front.

Ruth, holding Joshua's hand, lowered herself into the water and found it up to her knees immediately. It was cold and came straight into her clogs, so that her feet, already very damp, were completely sodden. Enoch was standing on the far side with an outstretched hand, and Shep was barking his encouragement, but Ruth felt that she was unstable. For a moment, she thought of going back, but knew that sooner or later she would have to cross.

'I'll be alreet,' she said to Joshua. 'Let go of me 'and.'

As Joshua released her hand, she moved into midstream and gingerly placed one foot after another. The current seemed very strong now, and her feet were sodden and cold. Searching for another foothold under the water, she felt her right foot sink into a hole whose bottom was much deeper. Her foot was suddenly trapped inside it and, wrenching it free, she felt it leaving her clog. Pulling her leg free of the hole and the clog, she lost her balance and fell into the foaming water. For a few seconds, she lay flat across the stream bed, instinctively drawing her legs to her body; and finding a new foothold, she pushed her head above the water and drew a deep breath of air into her lungs.

The first thing she saw and heard was Shep barking in desperation at her disappearance. Enoch was there too, shouting at her to reach out to him. Joshua, on the other side of the bank, was calling her to come back to his side. Further back, Marion was running over the rocks with Jim, shouting, 'Ruth, Ruth; get up, lass.' As Jim reached the bank of the stream, he pushed Joshua aside and let himself down quickly, pulling Ruth towards him. Picking her up, he placed her across his body and carried her in his two arms back to the bank.

Marion was deeply worried but calm enough. She knew Ruth was a strong girl who could survive a ducking. But she had little idea how much further they would be walking that day or how Ruth would survive clothes which were wet through in storm conditions. Ruth was shocked and frightened but managed a grateful smile to Jim and Marion. Looking down, she realised that only the clog on her left foot had survived the ducking.

'But Marion, I'll never be able to walk wi'out me clog,' said Ruth.

'Well, I'll say that's true enough,' said Marion, looking mournfully at Jim, who knew she was challenging him to grope in the stream for the missing clog.

Jim looked at Ruth and at the stream, and back to Marion. Just as he decided to wade in, Shep's bark caught everyone's attention. Fifty yards down stream, where it began to rush over the edge of the cliff, Shep was barking at the clog as it hurtled towards the waterfall. As his bark resounded across the rocks, Enoch realised that he was about to jump in and ran a high risk of being carried down the waterfall, a drop of several hundred feet. But

Enoch and Shep try to save Ruth

just as he whistled to Shep to 'Sit!', the dog leapt into the stream and disappeared into its rushing, white-capped waves. Enoch, calling Joshua to follow him, sprinted to the spot from which Shep had leapt, to find him swimming against the current with the clog held between his teeth. As the swollen water teemed around him, Shep desperately paddled as fast as he could, never letting go of the clog, but being swept bit by bit towards the fall.

Enoch and Joshua could see that Shep would be drawn over the edge in no time unless one of them waded in to catch him.

''Ere, 'old me 'and, Joshua,' said Enoch, as he stepped off the rock into the stream, leaning over to where Shep was treading a losing battle against the water. Bending over, he just managed to grab Shep by the collar and pulled him, with his teeth still clenched around the clog, towards the bank. Holding Joshua's hand, he pulled them both back up onto the rocks, only to see Shep rush off with the clog, wagging his tail as he ran towards Ruth.

'That were a near 'un,' said Joshua. 'Tha' was nearly a gonner.'

'Aye, and then tha'd be in a right pickle wi' no one to get thee to Edale,' said Enoch, as he surveyed his dripping trousers.

The two boys were soon joined by Eric Naylor and Judd Ackroyd, who, leaving his hammer with Ruth and Marion, had rushed over to prevent Enoch himself being swept into Kinder Downpour. They were relieved to find a dripping but still cheerful Enoch, who strode back to the point at which he thought the marchers should be crossing the stream. Speaking to Ruth, for once with a smile on his face, he said, 'Well, we'd best get on, or thee and me'll be frozen over.'

By this time, about twenty of the marchers, Jess Midgeley amongst them, had converged on the stream crossing. Jess was desparately concerned for Ruth, but could see that it would be best for her to resume the march as soon as she had found her feet. Once Enoch had seen her with two clogs on, and with his own trousers wet through, he wasted no time in striding through the stream again, closely followed by Joshua. Jess Midgeley now resolved to stay as close to Ruth as possible, and bent down to pick her up.

'Nay, Dad, I'll be alreet this time,' said Ruth, now surrounded by a group of twenty marchers and embarassed to be needing help.

'No tha' never will, lass,' said Jess, moving to pick her up. But Ruth was determined to cross on her own two feet, all the more so as more marchers came up to the stream bank and witnessed her plight. Jess knew his daughter well enough to leave her alone, but insisted on crossing first and giving her a hand as she waded over a second time. Once she had crossed successfully the crowd around Ruth took this as their cue and followed across the stream in single file, immediately picking up the trail blazed by Enoch at the front, with Jess and Ruth close behind him.

By this time Frank Sykes had reached the stream, closely followed by the two Oldham marchers who faithfully carried the Charter, now wrapped in a blanket which was soaked through.

'Go carefully, lads, an' tha'll be alreet. It's 'appen two feet deep and no more,' he said.

He watched them wade through the stream and stayed to count the two hundred or so marchers who had stayed with the march up the scree and over the top. He realised that nearly three times that number must have turned back and guessed that some would still be struggling in the peat bog. He hoped grimly that those he counted as friends would get back to their wives and homes unmolested by the soldiers. After a period of ten minutes had elapsed with no sign of another marcher, he crossed the stream himself and vowed to ensure that the whole column now stayed together and reached Edale in safety.

A mile to the front, Enoch and Joshua, with Shep at their heels, were setting a brisk pace along the track which continued to skirt the cliff edge, but now turned south. The storm had blown itself out and Enoch was determined to dry his trousers out by creating as much of a breeze as his short pace would allow. Shep, still thoroughly pleased with his exploit of saving the clog, ran back and forth between the two boys and Jess and

Ruth, who followed them at about a hundred yards.

'Keep this up and we'll be at Jacob's Ladder in ten minutes,' said Enoch.

'An' what then?' said Joshua.

'Why, we'll be down to Edale in 'alf an hour.'

As they pressed on along the track, it reached a crest dotted with a series of high rocks and then began a gradual incline. In the space of a few hundred yards, the incline funnelled into a steep valley, with a stream gushing through it. As they walked down the incline and came closer to the stream, they could make out a very steep footpath which followed its descent.

'There it is, Jacob's Ladder,' said Enoch. 'An' watch it, Joshua, or Shep'll trip you and 'ave you falling faster n' tha' wants to go.'

'Aye, likely 'e will,' said Joshua. 'An' that's a fall I'd rather not 'ave.'

Ruth could see that the two boys were well ahead of her and Jess and rapidly falling out of view as they descended the steep valley. Shep was finding it increasingly difficult to keep running between them as the distance lengthened. Although Ruth was still wet through, she had recovered from the shock of falling into the stream and found, like Enoch, that walking quickly was the best way of drying out. The sky was now clearing and there was even a hint of blue.

'Come on, Dad, let's catch 'em up,' said Ruth.

'Nay, lass, there's more than two 'undred behind us. I'd like to hold that Enoch back or they'll be lost.'

'I'll run on, Dad, an' tell 'em to wait, while you stay 'ere an' wait for't rest.'

She glanced at him briefly, and not finding disapproval, ran ahead towards the boys. As she caught up with them at where the stream ran over the cliff, the clouds cleared further and she could see down into the valley bottom. A pattern of green fields, farmhouses, trees and small lanes opened up before them.

'Aye, that's Edale, right enough,' said Enoch, proud to display his knowledge of what seemed like another country.

'Eee, 'ave never seen owt so green,' said Ruth. 'It's beautiful.'

'An' just where's this barn o' your cousin's then?' said Joshua.

''Appen two mile from where stream bottoms out after this waterfall.'

'An' 'ow long'll that tak us?'

'What, us and Shep, or your mob?'

Joshua looked back towards the head of the valley where about twenty marchers had now gathered round Jess and more were walking or stumbling towards him from the top of the moor.

'Dad says we should wait 'ere and not get so far ahead,' said Ruth. 'They'll 'ave no idea where to go when they get t' bottom 'o, this stream.'

Shep had his ears pricked up and wanted to dash ahead, but Enoch whistled him to 'Sit!' and reluctantly sat on a rock himself. Joshua and Ruth sat down too, both drinking in the lush scene before them.

'This is grand. If I were warm enough, I could sit 'ere forever,' said Ruth.

'Aye, it's a bit o' paradise alreet till tha' starts to farm it.'

'Oh, and what then?' said Ruth.

'First, tha'll have the devil's job to find land because it's all owned by t'Duke o' Devonshire, and if His Lordship's bailiff rents it to thee, tha'll 'ave to pay 'alf tha' crop to 'im. Our Nelly and 'er Jack are fair skint tho' they farm fifty acres an' more.'

By this time, Jess Midgeley had assembled about fifty marchers around him, including the Oldham men carrying the Charter; and knowing that Frank Sykes was bringing up the rear, he set off to join the children. Once they reached them, they could see the last group coming over the top of the moor, and Jess gave the word to Enoch to set off down Jacob's Ladder.

The very steep track turned back and forth every six feet or so as it wound its way down into the valley. Used mainly by shepherds and a few travellers passing from Edale into Lancashire, at some points it could hardly be seen. Enoch twisted and turned down the track, springing like a goat from one circuit to another, leaving Ruth and Joshua gasping behind him. Further up the path, the marchers moved slowly, quite unaccustomed to such a precarious route, and many stumbling as they climbed down. The descent was most difficult for the men carrying the Charter, who still managed to carry it from both ends of the pole.

Halfway down, Ralph Murphy, dependant on his walking stick, slipped badly and fell a good six feet from one section of the path to another. Jess Midgeley, walking below him, caught him as he fell and helped him stand up, the worse for wear.

'Nay, Ralph,' said Jess, 'tha' mustn't tumble into Edale wi' tha' bones broken. We want thee in London yet.'

'Don't worry about me, Jess Midgeley,' said Ralph, cleaning the mud off his clothes. 'I'll get to London all right. It's thee I'd worry about.'

Jess's face betrayed nothing, but when thanks were due, he expected them; and Ralph's comment seemed strange. He began to think he would have been happier if the Todmorden group had numbered one less. But as he looked down the track, his heart rose as the green fields of Edale beckoned like a haven. He wondered how far ahead lay the farm of Enoch's cousin and what kind of welcome they could possibly give to over a hundred rough marchers.

Enoch, Ruth and Joshua were still well ahead of the main body of marchers but, as Jess guessed, just in shouting range. Using his strong voice to the full, he

shouted the names of the children in turn, and added
Shep into the bargain. It was the dog that heard him
immediately and within three minutes came running
up to him.

'Bring your master back, lad,' he said as Shep
immediately dashed back to Enoch.

But it was an unnecessary instruction as Ruth and
Joshua had also recognised their father's voice, and the
three children halted to await his arrival. Catching up
with them, he asked Enoch:

'How far to tha' cousin's, lad?'

''Appen two mile.'

'An' 'ow long to walk it?'

'Maybe half an hour for me an' Shep; longer wi'
your lot.'

'An' you reckon your cousin and 'er 'usband'll not
turn us out?'

'Our Nelly turn you out? I doubt it. She were a
piecer in a mill at Glossop 'erself and she knows what
you're on about.'

'And 'er 'usband?'

'Well, 'e's a Derbyshire man, but not so bad for one
o' them. Mind you, 'e's got to keep in wi' Duke like, for
that's where 'e gets 'is farm from.'

Jess was more and more impressed with Enoch's
grasp of politics as well as moorland geography. He
could see they had little choice but to ask Nelly and her
Jack for a minimum amount of shelter for the night.

'Will tha' run on, lad, then, and ask 'em if they'll let two 'undred men, one woman and three children spend the night i' their fields or barn?'

'Aye, reet enough. An' we'll come back and meet you at the first bridge across the river. Are you coming then?' he nodded to Ruth and Joshua.

All three set off further down the farmtrack and towards the east of the valley. Ruth and Joshua were now tired through and through, and Ruth was only just beginning to dry out, but the thought of a possible welcome in a farmhouse – or its barn – gave them enough energy to keep up with Enoch. They were buoyed, too, by the sheer beauty of the valley, so much greener and lusher than the darker, harsher outlines of the Calder Valley at home.

After little more than half an hour, they came to a gate in the dry stone wall which ran alongside the track, and saw a low-lying farmhouse of grey stone at the other end of the field. There were sheep and signs that a hay crop had been taken. Shep showed every sign of setting out to round up the sheep but was kept back by a sharp whistle from Enoch.

The door was half-open and no sooner had Enoch put his head round it than he disappeared into the embrace of his cousin Nelly, who clearly regarded him as more of a young brother than a cousin. Nelly was auburn-haired and had a friendly face, but watching her grasp Enoch to her, Ruth saw a look of deep depression in her eyes.

'Well, Enoch lad, tha's come at a fine time. Duke's men 'ave takken us 'ay crop out o' t'barn 'cause we were backward wi' t'rent. God knows 'ow we'll get throught winter.'

Her husband, Jack, who had a dark face and short black beard, looked on from a high-backed chair with a sheep's fleece laced into it, from the side of a peat fire. Joshua could see that he was still a young man but that he seemed to be looking at Enoch with some dislike.

'Or through t'night for that matter, but I suppose that's what tha've come for,' Jack added, looking in a surly way at the three children.

'Aye, an' we've brought some marchers with a right big banner from Manchester way, what are walking to Lunnon.'

'An' are these childer two on 'em? Why, tha's wet through, lass!' said Nelly, looking at Ruth.

'Drying out now,' said Ruth, looking down at her dress.

'Well, we'll 'ave to finish the job for tha'. An' 'ow many more of you are there?'

'Me dad and Mr Sykes has brought about two 'undred over t'moor,' said Ruth, not wishing Enoch to attract the blame.

'Two 'undred over Kinder Scout! What about t'bogs, and t'scree and Jacob's Ladder?'

'Well, there at t'bottom o'ladder now,' said Enoch. 'In fact, there 'alf a mile away and I said 'appen they could sleep in thy barn and fields.'

'Oh you did, did yer?' said Jack from his chair by the fire. 'Well, 'appen they can give us a wide berth and get on their way since they've got to get to Lunnon.'

'Nay, Jack, that'll never do. Wi' this lass wet through and 'alf 'on 'em wi' sprained ankles, I'll be bound. Tha' cannot send 'em away. An' what wi' our barn being empty.'

'Our barn's empty through no fault of our own. It's not for a regiment of Chartists, for that's what they are, I'll be bound.'

'Jack, just for a night. Them Chartists is th'only 'ope for lads and lasses in t'mills. It's alreet for thee, tha's not worked twelve 'our a day in t'dust and noise of a mill. Tha's only known t'fields of Edale. We'll get 'em off by seven in t'morning.'

'Please tha' sen, but don't blame me if Duke's bailiff comes and throws us off t'farm. Chartists! That'd really finish us.'

Enoch looked questioningly at Nelly. Could he invite Jess to bring the marchers to the farm or not? Nelly knew that Jack would not put up further resistance but would maintain a surly face, perhaps coming round later.

'Aye, go on, you two lads,' she said, nodding them out of the door. 'But you, lass, stay 'ere an' we'll see what we can do for thee.'

Further back up the valley, Jess was waiting on the track with over fifty men, and more were straggling in by the minute. He knew that they would not be able to muster the energy to cross into the next valley beyond Edale, and if they had no shelter at the farm of Enoch's cousin, most of the men would simply refuse to go on. He was more than relieved to see Enoch and Joshua walking back towards him, with Shep dashing ahead.

'Yer alreet,' said Enoch. 'Nelly'll put you up, and 'er Jack won't stop it.'

Jess did not pause to consider the implications of this, but said simply: 'Well done, lad; that's grand.'

Turning round to the group of marchers, including Marion and Jim, who now surrounded him, he said, 'Well, you 'eard; we've got shelter for t'night, thanks to this lad. Enoch, wil'ta tak us there, and Joshua, will you stay 'ere to show Mr Sykes and the lads where we're going? Come on, let's be off.'

As they followed Enoch down the track to his cousin's farm, Jess realised what a bedraggled lot they were, and what an impression they could expect to make on their hosts. Though none were as soaked as

Ruth had been, they were all thoroughly wet; most had streaks of mud over their clothes, and some were limping badly. Alan and Jebb were again carrying the Charter strung on the pole between them, but trudged along as if it were a burden they would rather forget. Marion and Jim were amongst the few who still had some energy left, and Marion asked Enoch: 'An' 'ow's Ruth then?'

'Oh, Nelly'll 'ave wrapped 'er up warm by now. Don't worry about 'er.'

When they finally trooped into the farm, they found Nelly standing outside the door of the big barn, with Ruth at her side dressed in a calico dress that was too big for her. But her smile to Marion showed that she was dry and glad to see her companions.

'Well then,' said Nelly as soon as the marchers appeared, 'this is t'barn an' tha' can make best of it. There's water in t'well and a pail or two about. I've no food, mind, an' tha' mun keep clear o' t'dairy barn and sheep pen.' Turning to Ruth and looking at Jess, she added: 'That'll be tha' dad then.'

'Aye, and a right proud one today, missis. She's fair done 'er bit for t'Charter today what wi' screes and streams an' falling in. But I see we should thank thee for keeping her warm.'

'Well, the rest of you seem pretty wet, but there's not much I can do about that. But Ruth an' t'other childer can sleep wi' me in the 'ouse tonight.' Seeing that Ruth and Joshua looked uncertain, she added, 'That is, if it suits them.' Ruth had been looking at Marion and wanted to get her included in the group to sleep inside.

Nelly saw the look and added, 'Oh, and you too if tha' like. Ruth's told me about thee. Marion, isn't it?'

With Marion included, the children accepted Nelly's offer, staying outside to see the rest of the marchers arrive. It was another hour before Frank Sykes brought up the rear and followed the last straggler across the gate. Before long, the farmyard and barn were turned into a giant bivouac site, like a badly equipped regiment on the move. Most of the men had some bread and cheese left and soon brought out what little they had. They had been relying on supporters of the Charter to feed them en route, never imagining that they would be stranded in a remote farm in the Derbyshire hills. Frank and Jess conferred between themselves and with the few leaders of the other contingents to have made it across the moor. They realised that to avoid a mutiny, they would have to get everybody moving in good time in the morning – by seven o'clock at the latest.

For Ruth and Joshua, it was a great relief to find they could lie on a blanket on the floor of an attic in the house and realise that the day was behind them. What was more, Shep was quiet and finally lying down beside his master. Ruth thought about her mother and wondered how she would feel if she could see her children now. *Unhappy*, she thought, and *Just as bad as she expected.* But the truth was, it might be bad, but it wasn't so bad, and they might even be able to carry on tomorrow. She wondered why she seemed to hear footsteps on the stairs and a door open and close, but gave up trying to answer the question as she finally fell asleep.

CHAPTER 6

THE ESCAPE FROM BLACK SAM

It was the angry bark of the dogs that woke Ruth and Joshua just as light was breaking the next day. For a moment, Ruth thought it must be Shep fighting with one of Nelly's farm dogs, but as she leaned forward and put her face to the window she could see a dozen men each handling three hunting hounds.

'Josh lad, look 'ere,' she cried, pulling her brother's hand from the other end of the blanket. As Joshua wiped the sleep from his eyes and looked through the glass, he was terrified to see the men eyeing the farm as the hounds pulled at their leashes. They looked very like the dogs which had torn the flesh from his ankle on Langfield Common a year ago.

Enoch, who had been sleeping on a sheepskin with Shep next to him on the floor, came up to the window to join them.

'By God, that's Jack wi'em,' he cried, as he saw Nelly's husband, Jack, stooped and speaking to one of the men.

No sooner had he spoken than Nelly rushed into the room in her nightdress, hair streaming down her shoulders, shouting, 'Get out o'ere as quick as tha' can. Jack left in t'middle o' neet an' 'e's back now wi' Duke's men. That's Black Sam, Duke's bailiff, what 'e's talking to. They'll be driving t'lot o' you out wi' them 'ounds. Quick now. Keep them close to you, Marion.'

Nelly led Marion and the children down the stairs and across to the kitchen window to see if they could break out safely. The Duke's men were still looking over the stone wall which surrounded the farmyard and across to the barn. About a hundred of the marchers had camped out roughly in the yard, and another fifty were in the barn. Ruth could see that Jack was still talking to Black Sam, a huge man with a dark beard who looked as if he would gladly launch his hounds on the marchers. All over the yard, men who had been lying exhausted from the previous day's march were rising from the ground as they were wakened by the barking of the dogs. A handful of those who had been sleeping in the barn came to the door and looked out cautiously. Ruth and Joshua could see that their father and Frank Sykes were amongst them.

Nelly, who had seen Black Sam snatch the hay from their barn, could see that all the marchers were in terrible danger. She knew that he would not hesitate to unleash the hounds when he judged the moment right, and she had a sinking feeling that it was her husband who had brought Sam back to the farm. Looking through the window with the children and Marion, she said:

'We've got to warn 'em. Black Sam means to set his dogs on, no mistake; an' the sooner they start running, the better. But we need time to get everyone 'out 'o 'ere.'

''Appen we can distract 'em,' said Marion, who had been scouring the crowd in the yard for the face of Jim Knotts.

'Well, I'll send Shep out to do 'is tricks,' said Enoch, 'an' let's see if some of them big dogs don't get distracted.'

'Out there, lad,' said Enoch, opening the door, as Shep scampered into the middle of the yard, sensing the danger and smelling the hounds as he ran. Two high-pitched whistles from Enoch brought him to a halt; one low-pitched whistle set him off running in circles; three sharp whistles had him sitting up begging as the marchers looked on with wonder. As Shep performed, Black Sam's men could feel the hounds pulling ever more strongly at their leashes. Their harsh barking grew louder as their frustration at Shep's antics reached boiling point. Suddenly one of the keepers lost control of the leash holding three of the hounds. They dashed over to Shep, who turned and ran, running through the marchers, over a stone wall on the far side of the yard and into the field beyond. Several of the other hounds sprang free and joined in the chase. Enoch quickly followed them. Nelly, seeing that the ruse had distracted at least some of the dogs, rushed out of the kitchen door shouting,

'Lads, tha's not got a moment. You'd best be off this minute or there'll be no quarter. Jess, for tha' childer's sake, get them out this minute.'

Black Sam had still not spoken, but enraged by the false trail laid for the dogs, he now shouted at the marchers:

'Every one of you is trespassing on the land of the Duke of Devonshire. Give yourselves up and you'll get a fair trial. If you walk out across this farm, these dogs'll be on tha' legs and at tha' backs.'

Jess and Frank Sykes looked at each other: they could not afford to let the march collapse here, and fail to deliver the Charter to O'Connor in Nottingham. They nodded to each other.

'Run for it, lads,' cried Frank, as he dashed from the barn doorway towards a gate in the stone wall on the south side of the yard.

'Quick, over 'ere, Ruth and Joshua,' shouted Jess as they looked warily out of the kitchen door. The two children and Marion ran over to the barn door and immediately joined Jess in following Frank out of the south gate of the yard. As they ran, most of the marchers

Holding off Black Sam

poured out through the same gate with no more than a dozen walking diffidently towards Black Sam. The hounds were confused by the cross movements in the yard and were snarling and biting at the feet of anyone they came across. Those who stayed to give themselves up received the worst of the hounds' bites; half of the keepers were beside themselves trying to call their dogs off. The other half were trying to call back those who were still chasing after Shep. In the confusion, most of the marchers got away from the yard and streamed over the fields southwards from the farm, towards the hills that rose up on the south side of Edale. Frank could see that the bearers of the Charter were managing to keep pace with each other.

Black Sam glowered at his men and at Jack, and at the small troop of marchers that had surrendered to him.

'This 'as been a fine idea, Jack Gaunt. 'Is Grace'll be very pleased to know that we captured a good dozen of more than two 'undred marchers. Very pleased indeed. I'm sure 'e'd not want to throw off such a loyal tenant; quite sure.'

Black Sam's sarcasm was beyond Jack, but he had a sinking feeling that his betrayal of the marchers would cost him dear. As Nelly came over to them, she was holding back her tears as she said to him:

'Nay, Jack, I did na' marry thee for this.' Looking at Sam, she continued: 'I hope you're 'appy, Mr Sam, for what tha's done today. Them men and childer are doing nowt but what's right, and mean no 'arm. If thou sleep sound in tha' bed tonight, thou's an even worse man than I thought thee. Come in, Jack, look for no more favours from Mr Sam.'

'Yes, go in,' said Black Sam. 'I'll come and attend to thee next week, Gaunt. The rest of you'll be taken to Matlock to wait the magistrates' pleasure.' Saying this, he strode back to a horse held behind the wall, mounted and cantered off down the valley.

Running and staggering as best they could through the fields to the south side of the barn, the marchers eventually arrived at the River Noe, which was too deep to cross. At the point where they came up against the riverbank, they were spread out over a good quarter of a mile, searching desperately for a means to cross. Suddenly they heard barking in a thicket on the other side of the river: in seconds, Enoch and Shep emerged through the trees, as the four hounds who were still chasing them responded to their keepers' calls.

Enoch ran over to the bank on his side of the river, saying:

'It's that way. The crossing's that way. Two fields up, there are some logs across river and tha'll get across right enough.'

Jess Midgeley, with Ruth and Joshua close behind, was one of the last to arrive at the bank of the river. Looking for Frank Sykes amongst the marchers, he caught up with him pressing along the river towards the crossing which Enoch had found.

'This is a right mess, Frank,' he said. 'We're going to look a right 'appy crowd now as we march south.'

'Aye, and t'lads'll be wanting to turn back, Charter or no Charter.'

'Well, where is t'Charter, after this mauling?' said Jess.

They looked back amongst the crowd strung out along the riverbank. Frank could just make out Alan and Jebb, the two Oldham men who had been carrying the Charter on the previous day, and who had managed to drag it out of the barn whenthe dogs attacked. As he and Jess waited for them to catch up, he could see that they were both limping badly and were in no fit state to carry the additional burden.

'Ah see dogs got you then, lads,' said Frank. 'Is it bad then?'

'Aye, damn them. Ah can scarce walk, never mind carry t'Charter,' said Jebb.

'We'll 'ave to give it to someone else,' said Frank. 'Would one of your lot carry it, Jess?'

'Well, we can't ask Judd Ackroyd. 'Is 'ammer is that 'eavy – and we may need it the way things is going. I'd sooner ask Eric Naylor and Jim Knotts. Eric's small but strong enough, and we all know Jim's a right champion,' said Jess, knowing that Jim could hear him.

'Aye, that's right enough,' said Jim. 'A've got away clear enough from them dogs. Joshua, lad, go and find Eric and ask 'im to come up 'ere.'

Walking back down the straggling marchers, Joshua felt this must be what a defeated army looked like. Some were holding their ankles and wrists where the dogs had drawn blood, others were visibly white and exhausted from the strain of the previous day: all were hungry, and few greeted him with a smile. He found Eric Naylor amongst those who were furthest downstream from the crossing, looking despondently at the river.

'Eric, me dad's axing if tha'd carry Charter wi' Jim Knotts. Them Oldham lads 'as been bitten by t'dogs 'n' it's too 'eavy for 'em now.'

Taken aback, Eric said:

'Me, lad? Why me? Aren't they afraid I'd drop it in t'river or fall of a cliff wi' it?'

'No, it's you they want,' said Joshua, who was clear about his instructions.

'Well, if they're that serious, I'd better do it, lad,' said Eric. 'Let's get up to t'front then.'

Eric and Joshua rejoined Jess Midgeley and Frank Sykes at the river crossing, which was no more than three stout logs laid over the water. Jim Knotts was there with the Charter, sitting down alongside the weakened team from Oldham.

'There you are,' said Jim, looking doubtfully at Eric.

'Yes. I'm here right enough and ready to go, even wi' thee at t'other end of t'pole,' said Eric, smiling at Jim.

'That's settled then,' said Jess. 'Frank, let's get these lads on to t'other side and get on t'way to Nottingham. There's some as need a doctor even more than they need bread and ale.'

Over the next quarter of an hour, all the marchers crossed the stream and regrouped in the field beyond. Frank Sykes mustered enough energy to make a short speech castigating the keepers and traitors such as Jack Gaunt, but praising Nelly for her kindness. He said that Nelly had told Marion Rowley the previous night the rough direction of the route to Miller's Dale, the next valley to the south, and that Jim Knotts knew the way from Miller's Dale to Matlock for he'd worked at a mill in those parts.

The rest of that day and the next one were agony for the marchers. With almost no food left, they trudged across rough country to Miller's Dale, leaving the dark millstone grit rocks and stone walls of the Pennines for the white limestone of northern Derbyshire. They passed a few isolated limestone quarries on the hills and skirted villages nestling in the valleys, afraid now that their presence would make enemies rather than attract support.

In the long winding valley of Miller's Dale, they had felt the protection of the steep walls of the valley which seemed to shut out the dangers of the march and gave them seclusion amidst its dense woodland. In one hamlet close to the river, the owner of the public house had given them five giant Derbyshire cheeses which, divided up, became their first meal for more than a day. That night, they had slept in the woods and pressed on early next morning with Jim Knotts as guide, skirting past the Cressbrook mill where Jim had worked as a child-winder. Looking up at the cold but handsome building, Jim had contemplated ringing the mill bell and bringing all hands out to hear a call to strike and join the march. But Frank and Jess had talked him out of it in case it led to further harassment by millowners, landlords or magistrates. Their task now was simply to get the Charter to Nottingham, where they were to meet the other group of marchers.

It was a good half-day from Cressbrook to Matlock where there was a strong Chartist group. O'Connor had passed on the address of their leader, Alexander Tayburn, to Frank Sykes. Frank and Jess were praying that Tayburn would be able to provide them with a safe place to sleep and something to fill the marchers' stomachs. Jess went ahead into the town with Jim Knotts to search for Tayburn's house, found him easily enough and had been shown to a Sunday School building which belonged to a Methodist congregation, amongst whom there were many strong Chartists.

The school – where classes were given to more than three hundred children on Sundays – was big enough to accommodate all the marchers for a night. Members of the Methodist congregation had made soup in the evening and porridge in the morning, and given the marchers the strength to continue for one more day for the forty miles to Nottingham. Two doctors, who were members of the congregation, had been able to tend to the wounds inflicted by the dogs, but they had advised six of the marchers to stay behind under their care.

At night, the marchers had held intense discussions with the Matlock Chartists on whether Parliament would ever allow the vote to the common man who had failed to win it in the Reform Bill of 1832. The riots which had led up to the Reform Bill had raged over the north, and Matlock had been no exception. Alexander Tayburn's son argued that this was the last year for the Charter: failure this year would lead to much more serious rioting and arson next year. But the evening had ended on a note of harmony as Marion had found the strength to sing the Chartists' hymn, '*Britannia's Sons, Though Slaves Ye Be*', and there had been more than two hundred in the room to join in the chorus.

It was when both the arguments and the singing were over, and exhaustion had settled over most of the marchers sleeping on the Sunday School floor, that Enoch had risen from the floor, taken Shep in his arms, and quietly made for the door. Ruth had been thinking too hard to sleep easily and had just caught a glance of him as he began to open the door. Getting up herself, she woke Joshua, who followed her to the door. No sooner had Enoch and Shep stepped outside than they found Ruth and Joshua beside them.

'Enoch, what are you doing?' said Ruth.

'I'm off. A've got thee to Matlock. What more do tha' want?' said Enoch.

'But tha' can't leave now,' said Joshua. 'Tha's part of us, part o' t'march.'

'Besides,' said Ruth, 'we want Shep at Parliament to bark at them members and tell 'um summut.'

'Nay, that's thy dad's business, and Mr Sykes. That's not for me and Shep. We just wants us grass and us sheep, lad, don't we?'

'So we won't see you again, Enoch?' said Ruth, realising he was serious.

'An' we won't see Shep?' said Joshua.

'An' you'll not say goodbye to me dad?' added Ruth in wonder.

'No, I'll not,' said Enoch. 'Not that I won't say you're a good lass, and your brother's a good 'un too, but Shep and me are not one for farewells, so we'll be off. Come, boy, come.'

'Well, give us thy 'and at least,' said Ruth, stretching

out her own. Enoch looked surprised but took it and found the squeeze she gave it pleasant enough, before he took Joshua's more roughly and dropped it before turning and walking down the steps.

'Shall we really never see 'im again?' Joshua asked Ruth as they turned back into the Sunday School.

'Well, it won't be on this march, anyroad,' said Ruth. 'I could sleep standing up, 'am that tired. Let's think about it in t'morning.'

The porridge that had filled their bellies the next morning, and the brightness of the day, had done much to put thoughts of Enoch and Shep out of the minds of Ruth and Joshua. Their father and even Marion had seemed much less surprised than they had been; perhaps they had earmarked Enoch as a loner, and perhaps too they were glad not to have the responsibility of taking him through the uncertainties of Nottingham and London. But they knew they would never have got over Kinder Scout without him.

The journey from Matlock to Nottingham was over a fairly straight turnpike road where horse-drawn vehicles paid a toll, but pedestrians were free. It was a sunny day, and the speed of the march had picked up as they left the valleys of Derbyshire and came into the flatter country of Nottinghamshire. Although all the marchers were feeling weaker than when they left Manchester, and some with bandages were still hobbling from the attack by Black Sam's hounds, they knew that the arrival at Nottingham would be at least halfway to their goal.

It was close to dusk at about 6pm when they caught sight of the ruins of Nottingham Castle in the distance. It stood high on a hill overlooking the large town, but its gaping walls and collapsing parapets gave it a more sinister and awe-inspiring look than it could ever have had in the past.

'Whatever's 'appened to that castle, Dad?' said Joshua. 'It looks right ghostly from 'ere.'

'I can't tell thee, lad,' said Jess, 'but we'll find out soon enough when we meet Mr O'Connor and Mr Place.'

O'Connor had stipulated that the two groups of marchers – those who had gone through the towns and those who had gone over the moors – would meet in a field between the River Trent and the River Leen about half a mile from the castle, where he believed the local Chartists could help them camp. O'Connor regarded the Nottingham group as one of the best organised in the country and had every confidence in their support.

Like the bigger towns of Lancashire and the city of Manchester, Nottingham was expanding fast at this time. At the heart of its activity was the lace industry, which had once depended on the ability of dexterous hands to do fine needlework, but had come to be increasingly dependent on machinery which took work away from those hands and gave it to machine minders. For this reason, Nottingham had been one of the centres of the Luddite movement, and 'King Ludd', the most famous of the great machine breaking hammers, had been made in Nottingham. Judd Ackroyd's hammer, which had smashed machines in Halifax, was modelled on 'King Ludd'. Judd, for one, was glad to be in such a famous town, and O'Connor had good reason to expect strong support there.

Frank and Jess easily found the area on the river that O'Connor had in mind. Although most of the marchers were ready to drop from exhaustion, Frank persuaded them to walk or hobble the final mile to the meeting place. Ruth and Joshua were relieved to find that here they met smiles and cheers as they finished the day's march. It seemed unlikely they would be in danger here from soldiers, dogs or keepers.

The first sign of O'Connor's encampment was a white flag flying from a long pole which Ruth and Joshua caught sight of through the hedge of a field. Stopping to peer through the hedge, Ruth said:

''Ere they are, Josh. Looks like there's even summut to eat. See that smoke? They must be cooking.'

'Thank 'eaven for that. I could eat a log of wood, never mind our mam's oatcakes.'

'Well, tha's far enough from them, lad,' said Jess, overhearing their conversation. 'But it looks like we may fill tha' belly toneet.'

He was smiling with relief to see that O'Connor's group had arrived and had been able to camp unmolested. Although the marchers were standing, sitting or lying in groups about the large field, it looked as if most of the five hundred who had left Manchester with O'Connor had arrived at Nottingham.

Walking in the middle of the marchers, Ruth and Joshua followed the group into the main gate of the field. As they turned into it, they found their way barred by a long staff as a gruff voice said:

'Stand and deliver in the name of the Charter!'

Looking up, they saw Jethro Strongitharm doing guard duty on the gate.

'Jethro!' cried Joshua, 'tha' got 'ere afore us! 'Ow did tha' manage that? Tha' must 'ave 'ad a right nice stroll.'

'Well, lad, I won't say as 'ow it's been like fighting Boney but it 'as been a march, I'll tell you that. But you both look like this'll be the last yard tha' walk.'

'Yes, I'm fair ready to drop,' Joshua confessed. 'But not before I've seen what's cooking over yonder.'

'Well then, I'll let thee both in,' said Jethro, 'but only if you promise to bring an old soldier a bit of summut to fill 'is belly.'

'We might,' smiled Ruth, pushing Jethro's staff aside and saying: 'It depends what we find.'

Held back by this conversation, the children could see that their father and Frank Sykes were walking ahead to the flagpole where a small group was assembled in discussion. As they came closer, they could see that the group included O'Connor with his big beard and Francis Place with his top hat. They saw the two leaders take their father and Frank warmly by the hand and heard them quickly ask the whereabouts of the Charter. Turning round, Jess pointed to Eric Naylor and Jim Knotts who were amongst the last of their group to turn into the field, still carrying the Charter on a pole between their shoulders. O'Connor looked visibly relieved and strode over to meet them. As he did so, he saw Ruth and Joshua and stopped in his tracks to greet them:

'Well, wonderful! Here they are! The ones who turned the cannons' fire in Manchester. Still marching! And how was your journey? Your father tells me not so easy.'

'Well,' said Ruth, thinking quickly, 'there's not much left of us feet, clogs or ankles; but otherwise, we're 'ere alreet.'

'An' there's not much in us bellies,' added Joshua with a smile.

'Well, what we've got to eat, we'll all share,' said O'Connor. 'And I'm really glad to see thee. You'd better go over to the fire and see what the smoke's all about.'

Ruth and Joshua were happy enough to stake their claim for whatever lay cooking under the smoke and, forgetting how tired they were, went off in the direction of the largest of the campfires. Just as they parted from O'Connor, they could see his face light up as he saw the arrival of the delegation of Nottingham Chartists led by his close friend Francis Drayman. Walking towards the largest of the fires, they hardly noticed the slight figure of Ralph Murphy, still carrying his twisted walking stick, moving towards the flagpole where the leaders were meeting.

CHAPTER 7

ARREST THE RINGLEADERS!

As the light of the day faded, the flames of the fires appeared to burn more brightly and most of the marchers were attracted to one or other of the fires. As Ruth and Joshua walked in the direction in which O'Connor had pointed them, they found a group of about thirty marchers standing, sitting or crouching around the flames. These were faces which they did not recognise since they were part of the group which had marched through the towns. But they were friendly enough and could see from the children's muddy clothes that they must have walked over the moors.

'Well, you two, ready for some o' this, then?' said a young man with a bright red shirt and baggy trousers who was stirring a large pot of porridge.

'Or 'appen tha'd like an oatcake or two?' said an older man with a scarf tied round his neck but reaching up to his nose as he held a frying pan in each hand, both of which warmed six oatcakes.

'Well, what about both?' asked Joshua hopefully as he eyed the two cooks.

'Joshua, tha'd better ask for one or t'other or tha'll get neither,' said Ruth.

'Aye, well said, lass,' said the porridge stirrer. 'Tha' mun never ask for more na' what the Lord 'as made available to each on us and what Matt – that's meself – can stir in a single pot.' Looking at the children more carefully, he added:

'But I will say there's more mud on thee than us, an' tha'must 'ave 'ad a rough time on t'tops.'

'Well, it were a bit rough up there,' said Joshua, speaking with the voice of experience.

'But we 'ad some good friends what kept us out o't bogs and saved us from t'cliff edge and gave us a bed… well, anyroad, until dogs came for us,' said Ruth more thoughtfully.

'What dogs?' said a small voice from the other side of the fire.

Looking across the flames, Ruth was surprised to see a girl of her own age, crouching down on her knees looking attentively at her. Although her face was alert, it was also grimy, and she was wearing a ragged dress and no shoes. Ruth was surprised to see another child there but answered calmly enough.

'Why, Black Sam's 'ounds what they use for 'unting foxes an' deer were what were set on us,' said Ruth.

'An' 'ave tha' got scars to show it?' said the voice.

'Well, Joshua an' I were lucky,' said Ruth, 'but there were some o' men what we had to leave in Matlock what were that badly mauled.'

'Eeh, ah'd like to see them scars,' said the small voice.

'Now that's a wonderful thing,' said Matt, stirring his pot. 'The young lady wants to see a scar or two, and just what a dog can do to a man. Well, that's curiosity for you. But shouldn't you three get to know each other. This is Ellie from the great city o' Nottingham where they make the finest lace in the world, and this is... well... I don't rightly know...'

'I'm Ruth and this is Joshua,' said Ruth, uncertain as to whether she should go and shake Ellie's hand.

Ellie felt no such uncertainty but came round and stood beside the children, looking at them carefully. She evidently liked what she saw for she said quickly: 'Ah see mud but no blood. Let's sit down.'

Ruth and Joshua were used to the bluntness of Todmorden speech, but this directness was something new. But Ruth particularly liked it. As Ellie sat down beside her, she saw that her hair, which hung in strands down her cheeks and neck, though unkempt and dirty, was a light blonde. Ruth marvelled that anyone would allow a girl of her age to run so wild, but any further thoughts were interrupted as Matt offered porridge to anyone with a plate to take it. Ruth and Joshua had managed to keep the small tin plates their mother had tied into their bundles as they left Todmorden and were delighted to see a large spoonful of porridge placed on them.

As the group surrounding the fire became absorbed in the scanty food being served by Matt and his colleague, they scarcely noticed the arrival of O'Connor and the leaders of the Nottingham Chartists.

Looking up from his pot, Matt was the first to see them. 'Mr O'Connor,' he cried, 'will tha' not 'ave a plate of porridge for tha' tea?'

'Not yet, brother, not yet,' O'Connor replied. 'We've still got to sort out tomorrow with these lads here.'

Raising his eyes from his scoop of porridge, Joshua noticed that the Nottingham leaders were a group of three and that O'Connor and Place were now talking to them in quiet tones. But he was puzzled to see Ralph Murphy on the fringe of the group, probably just within earshot.

'Well, do you think tha' you can bring out a good twenty thousand then?' said O'Connor to the group.

'Twenty thousand might be a bit on the high side, Feargus,' said a well-dressed man, standing a little below six feet, with spectacles and a top hat. 'But it'll be over by ten, and they'll be there for as long as you can hold 'em with your speech.'

'Aye, tha's right there, Mr Wilson,' said a much smaller man, dressed in a rough grey overall which came down to his knees. 'Nottingham folk'll listen to Mr O'Connor for as long as 'e can find words for 'is voice.'

'An' it'll not just be t'lace makers, Jack,' said the third man, whose dirty appearance and unkempt fair hair suggested he came from a rougher background than either of the other two. 'There's canalmen, an' porters what work for sixpence a day, an' night-soil men, an' servants that daren't speak their mind, and then there's us brewers on castle hill that yer'll be remembering fro' your visit last year. An' there's not a one o' t'brewers what won't come out.'

'Aye, ah know that well enough, Davy, and you'll 'ave an 'and in that. But will we be safe at Exchange Square – or will they bring the troops out if we come into the City? Perhaps tha' should bring t'lads out 'ere.'

'Or into t'grounds o' t'castle,' said Davy. 'It's been practically deserted since it were burned down. Tha' can do owt in there.'

'No, Davy,' said John Wilson. 'We want the maximum possible impact and the maximum disruption of business. We want the Lord Lieutenant to report to the Home Secretary that Nottingham is on fire again and won't settle for less than the Charter. We'll close down most o' t'lace mills as the lads walk out tomorrow.'

'Very well, that's settled,' said O'Connor in his usual decisive manner. 'When do we bring t'marchers in to meet your lads?'

'Leave at ten, and meet at the canal wharf at eleven,' said Wilson. 'That'll get us t'square at noon and we can start meeting then.'

O'Connor and Place nodded agreement to each other. 'Tomorrow at eleven then, but send your scouts out early,' said O'Connor. 'Now, won't you have some o' t'porridge an' oatcakes you sent out earlier?'

'No, Feargus, we'll leave that for you, as those who gave it intended,' said Wilson, whose Chartist organisation had collected oatcakes and porridge oats in a mass of small contributions to feed the marchers.

'Aye,' said Davy, 'they'd not want to see us downing it.'

Saying this, he looked across at the group to whom they were closest, took stock of the three children twenty yards away and called out:

'Ellie, lass; come 'ere this minute.'

'Why, Dad, what's up?' came the sharp answer.

'That food's not for thee, lass. There'll be summut for thee when tha' gets 'ome.'

'That'll not be much,' said Ellie to Ruth. 'There's never owt to eat in our cave.'

'Cave?' said Joshua. 'Tha' mean tha' lives in a cave?'

'Aye, me ducks, wi' 'undred other folk in t'caves on castle 'ill,' said Ellie. 'It's not so bad in summer but it don't 'alf freeze i' winter. Anyway, that's where we brew t'beer an' we'd never get by without that.'

'So tha's a beer brewer,' said Joshua, who was impressed, although his beer drinking had been limited to half a glass on special occasions.

'Aye, tha' could say that, since me dad's out o t'way for most o' week, organising for t'Chartists as he calls it. But I wonder. Any'ow, it's me what brews and sells most of what's sold from our barrels. Tha'd best come and see us tomorrow. We're just down by Journey to Jerusalem Inn.'

'An' what's tha' second name, Ellie?' said Joshua.

'Oh, Tinker,' she replied. 'That's what me grandad were, tha' sees, a tinker. But me and me dad 'ave settled down. No more travelling, just sat in a cave. Mind tha' come tomorrow.'

By midnight, the field where the marchers were camped had fallen quiet, and the noise of conversation arose from only a few small groups of huddled figures with blankets thrown round their shoulders, staring into the embers of the cooking fires. Most of the marchers lay stretched out where they had finished eating. Jethro had been replaced as guard on the gate to the field and had rejoined the Todmorden group. Ruth and Joshua were about a hundred yards away, sleeping close to the fire where they had met Ellie. Jess had talked late with O'Connor, Frank Sykes and the other leaders, who as a group now slept close to the flagpole in the middle of the field.

Ruth and Joshua both felt the cold. It was now mid-October and the autumn night already held the prospect of winter. As the night grew colder, they huddled together. But Ruth smiled to herself as she thought of Ellie, and looked forward to the chance of seeing her the next day. And then there was the prospect of London – with Parliament, the new Queen and the River Thames. She longed to see her mother, but only when she could tell her that she'd been to London and delivered the Charter to Parliament. Looking forward to the rest of the journey, and drawing heat from Joshua's body, Ruth finally drifted off to sleep.

It was the noise of the horses that woke Joshua. As dawn began to break, he heard the jingle of harnesses and shouts of command and, opening his eyes, saw a column of about fifty soldiers canter through the gate to the field.

'Ruth, Ruth, wake up,' he cried. 'We've got cavalry in t'field.'

Reluctantly opening her eyes, Ruth saw the column turning through the gate. They were in full dress uniform and had their cutlasses drawn. A figure at the gate, waving a long stick, seemed to be trying to stop them from entering the field. An officer at the front of the column, holding his cutlass above his head, was shouting at him.

'Get out of the way, man, damn you.'

'That's Jethro, Josh,' Ruth cried. ''E's going to be cut down! Let's get over there.'

As the two children ran the hundred yards to the gate, they saw the cavalry officer take a swipe at Jethro and then watched him fall, as the column slowed to a walk. By now, men were standing up all over the field, and a murmur of protest began to rise on all sides. Ruth and Joshua continued to run over to where Jethro had fallen. They found him on his back with the cavalry formed up about twenty yards away.

'Jethro, are tha' 'urt bad?' asked Joshua, bending over him.

'Nay, not so bad, lad. 'E turned his cutlass flat to 'it me, an' that's what knocked me flying.'

'Tha's not wounded then?' said Ruth.

'No blood, lass. Gi' us the crutch.'

The blow from the cutlass had separated Jethro from his crutch which lay a few feet away. Ruth passed it to him now, and letting it take his weight, Jethro pulled himself up. The soldiers were close by, but ignored

Jethro and the children. The officer in charge, having slowed his column down to a walk, led them towards the flagpole in the centre of the field. O'Connor and the other leaders were just being roused to see the column heading towards them.

The officer in charge, dressed in a captain's uniform, did not hesitate. Reining his horse to a halt close to the flagpole, he gave the command:

'Arrest the ringleaders!'

Ten of his men dismounted while the others drew their cutlasses and held them at the ready.

'Step forward, Feargus O'Connor, Francis Place, Ben Mather, Frank Sykes and Jess Midgeley.'

Not one of them moved, and each stood shocked but defiant in the cold dawn light.

O'Connor drew himself up to his full height. 'By what right do you arrest us?' he thundered.

'By right of a magistrate's warrant, Mr O'Connor, which specifies you and these other four men.'

'And on what charge?'

'Conspiring to disrupt the peace.'

'This has been no conspiracy. We plan to hold an open meeting in Exchange Square with some of our friends in Nottingham. Is this a conspiracy, Captain?'

'Sir Henry Fowler, the magistrate, will have something to say about that, and you will find he knows a good deal about it. But I'll not talk more now. Take these men.'

Those of the troop that had dismounted divided into pairs and, apparently recognising each of the leaders, grabbed them roughly from behind.

'You'll be walked to the courthouse in the Shire Hall, and you can plead your case there,' said the Captain.

'I'll plead my case to no one but the people and Parliament,' said O'Connor. Raising his voice, he shouted:

'Lads, they want to carry us off to gaol. Defend the gate, for they'll not get us through it with a hundred of you there.'

The full shock of the presence of the cavalry, the striking-down of Jethro and the apparent arrest of the leaders only now dawned on the mass of the marchers. A great murmur of protest went up from all corners of the field; some moved to the gate as O'Connor had instructed, others moved towards the threatened leaders and the cavalry.

Ruth and Joshua were still close to the gate with Jethro. They had been frightened by the spectacle of so many soldiers on horseback and the striking-down of Jethro, but relieved that the soldiers had let him stand up and had then ignored him. Their fears were heightened as they watched the column move towards the flagpole, for they both realised that their father was there with O'Connor.

'Joshua,' cried Ruth, 'Dad's over yonder where soldiers is going. We'd best go to 'im.'

'Nay, lass. Tha'd best stay 'ere,' said Jethro. 'There's going to be enough trouble over yon, and tha' dad wouldnot wish tha' to be in it.

'Well, looks like trouble's coming 'ere,' said Joshua, as a good third of the marchers followed O'Connor's call and converged on the gate. At the same time, the cavalry surrounded their captives and began to walk in the same direction.

Seeing the numbers approaching the gate, and the danger that his column would be cut off, the captain ordered his men to draw their cutlasses. But the column could move no faster than the speed of its captives, who were walking as slowly as their guards would allow, and they now held their cutlasses at their prisoners' backs.

Reaching the gate before the cavalry, a group of the marchers quickly formed a line across it. Ruth and Joshua were held back from joining it by Jethro's strong arms which now encircled them, and stood a few yards away from the path which the troops would take.

'Nay, tha'll stay wi' me,' he said. 'There's going to be trouble in that line.'

The captain was enraged to see the line blocking his troops' path. His orders were to deliver the ringleaders to the magistrates at Shire Hall within the hour, and he intended to carry them out. He did not give his men the order to slow down or come to a halt as they came up against the line of marchers. Ruth and Joshua watched in horror as the first three enormous cavalry horses trampled down the thin line of marchers strung across the gate. As their comrades went to pull them from under the horses' bellies, the next line of horses trampled them too, until there were a good twenty marchers caught up between the legs of the horses. By this time, more than a hundred marchers surrounded the troop, some of whom began to pull at the boots of the horsemen, only to find themselves pushed back at the point of a cutlass.

Jethro could see that his fears were being confirmed and pulled the children further away from what was fast becoming a violent mauling. Ruth was shouting to her father:

'Dad, are thee alreet? Where'll they tak tha'?'

Catching the sound of the only girl's voice in the tumult, Jess turned in her direction and saw his two children now struggling to be free of Jethro and come over to him.

'Lass, tha'd best stay out of this,' he called. 'We'll be alreet. There's still a law of some sorts 'ere. Stay wi' Jethro and Marion.'

He said no more as one of his guards jabbed him with his cutlass, saying in a gruff voice:

'Shut tha' mouth. Another word and this goes deeper.'

The marchers, on foot and unarmed, were no match for the mounted troop. Within a few minutes, the line across the gate had broken, and the cavalrymen were walking their horses through it with their prisoners still closely guarded. The marchers who had been trampled, and those who had been struck while attempting to rescue them, lay on the ground watching the troops' departure.

Ruth and Joshua looked at each other and at Jethro with forlorn faces. Their new friends made on the march were good to them, but without their father they would feel lost. Ruth felt that at the least she needed to see Marion and looked about the field to find her. Her eyes soon caught the top-hatted figure of William Steele, the journalist, who the children had last seen at the big meeting in Manchester. He noticed the children too and, skirting the wounded marchers, walked over to them.

'Hello, Ruth and Joshua. This is a terrible business. You've walked a long way to see this.'

'Aye, and they've takken our dad, now,' said Joshua, with tears in his eyes.

'Oh, your father was amongst those arrested?'

'Yes, there 'e is being dragged away,' said Ruth, pointing to the backs of the departing soldiers. 'He's one of 'em in second row.'

'What do you think, sir?' said Jethro. 'Will they send 'em to gaol?'

'That will be what they want to do,' said Steele. 'And Nottingham magistrates have a habit of getting what they want, and getting it quickly. But my newspaper will have plenty to say about this, and we might even get them out again.'

'But when?' said Ruth. 'An' will they be alreet when they come out? Won't they get sick in a damp dungeon? Will they chain 'em to t'wall?'

'Well,' said Steele, 'they won't feed them on roast beef and Yorkshire pudding, but they'll not starve, and I shouldn't worry too much about the chains.'

'Without them leaders, this march'll get nowhere,' said Jethro.

'I'm sure you're right there,' said Steele. 'And that's why I'm going to do everything I can to get them out. But where will you children go now? If the magistrates realise your father's got children here, they might even send a warrant for your arrest!'

Numbed by this thought, the children moved closer to Jethro and, as they did so, saw that Marion and Jim Knotts were running up to them.

'This is right bad,' said Marion, out of breath. 'Arresting your dad and t'rest – it's disgusting. As for that captain, I'd like to shoot 'im myself.'

'That's pluck for you,' said Steele, 'and I'm sure you're a good shot. But what about these two? They need to get out of the way for a few days.'

'Well, they've got no one except us 'ere,' said Marion.

'But we made a friend yesterday, Marion,' said Ruth. 'She wanted us to go and see 'er and 'er dad int' town.'

'An' who were she?' said Marion.

'She called hersel Ellie,' said Joshua. 'An' she lives in a cave.'

'In a cave!' said Marion. 'Wi' rats and spiders?!'

'No,' said Ruth. 'Wi' barrels o' beer, for that's what she an' her dad brew.'

Steele could see that Marion looked doubtful, but he was sure the children needed to lie low.

'Marion, the children could be in danger of arrest themselves. If there's someone in Nottingham that'll give them shelter, they should take it. Especially if it's in a place where the magistrates would never think of looking. Ruth and Joshua, do you know where this cave is?'

'Ellie said it were right under castle. Some'ow in t'illside.'

'Well, Marion and...' Steele looked at Jim, unsure of his name.

'Jim Knotts.'

'And Jim. Can I suggest you go with these two and try and find the cave and Ellie? Once you find her, leave the children if you can. You can see them daily to make sure they know what's happening. I'll keep you posted on my campaign.'

Jethro gave the final word of encouragement.

'Aye, 'e's right enough, Marion. Tha'd best tak 'em into t'town an' find this lass.'

'Well then, Ruth and Joshua, let's 'ave a good look

for your friend. But I'll be watching out for them rats and spiders.'

'Bye, Jethro,' said Joshua, looking up to the old soldier who he was always sorry to leave.

'Bye, children,' said Jethro. 'Tha'll still find me on guard duty, like as not, when tha' gets back.'

Marion and Jim and the children waved a goodbye and set out to find the caves and Ellie. William Steele began writing busily in his notebook.

They could see the ruined castle clearly as they left the field, and it served as their beacon. The walk away from the field took them first through the outskirts of the town where old farm cottages existed side by side with new. As they crossed the canal, they entered a maze of narrow streets of older houses where children, cats and dogs, and men with bales on their shoulders jostled for position. Everywhere they heard words and phrases that were close to their own but which were somehow spoken differently. Peeping inside one of the houses with an open door, Joshua could see a woman and a man at work on machines, producing finer and fancier material than any he had ever seen.

Eventually, they found themselves close to a sheer rock face with an inn nestling at its feet. Looking up, they saw the old battlements of the castle rising above the rock.

'It must be close to 'ere,' said Ruth. 'For Ellie said caves were in t'rock under t'castle.'

'Well, yon inn looks right enough for me,' said Jim. 'I'd swap it for a cave any time. The Journey to Jerusalem, eh, not a bad name.'

'Come on, Jim, we're not worried about your entertainment now,' said Marion. 'Let's get over there and ask for t'brewers. They should know their whereabouts right enough.'

The inn was built out from the rock face and seemed to be almost a part of it.

'It's almost falling down,' said Joshua.

'Aye, lad; not long to go,' said Jim.

'But it looks so old. It must 'ave been there for centuries,' said Ruth.

'An' what's stood that long might last a few more,' said Marion.

A group of half a dozen horses were tied up outside the inn, and two young teenage boys were brushing them down.

'Jim, go and ask them way t'caves,' she said. 'We don't all want to be seen asking t'way when we're trying to 'elp these two lie low.'

Jim went over to the boys, who pointed further down the massive rock; and Marion and the children followed the direction on the other side of the road. They met Jim at a point just outside sight of the inn and round the corner of the rock face. Standing fifty yards back from the cliff, they could see several openings in the rock over a space of about a hundred yards. A roughly dressed boy, carrying a small keg on his shoulder, came out of one of them.

'Looks like we're on the right lines,' said Jim.

'Let's go and ask 'im if 'e knows Ellie.'

Marion spoke to him as their paths crossed. ''Ullo, young lad. Dos't a know a young lass by t'name of Ellie?' said Marion.

'Ellie Tinker? Aye, I know 'er right well. She's right enough but me dad says 'e's not so sure about 'er brewing. Tha'll find 'er in that cave yon,' and he pointed to a cleft in the rock about fifty yards away.

Reaching it, they found themselves facing a canvas flap on which was written: TINKERS' ALES: THE CASTLE'S BEST. Jim pushed the flap aside and led the way in. It was difficult to see anything of the immediate area behind the canvas, but a glow of light came from round a corner a few yards away.

'Who's there?' cried a young voice, which Ruth and Joshua recognised.

'It's us. Ruth and Joshua,' said Ruth. 'Where are you?'

Ellie appeared round the corner of the rock chamber. Outlined by the glow of the lamp behind her, with her fair hair tumbling down her shoulders, she looked like a strange spirit rather than flesh and blood.

'Well, if it's not the 'eroes of the march. Come to see Ellie in 'er den, 'ave you?'

'Ellie,' said Ruth, can you 'elp us. Me dad an' t'other leaders have been arrested an' carried off by t'cavalry. They'll put 'em in jail, like as not, an' they may drag us there too.'

'We've got to 'ide for a few days,' added Joshua. 'In case they come back for us.'

Ellie looked from them to Marion and Jim.

'An' are tha' friends wanting to 'ide too?' she asked, looking doubtfully at the adults.

'No, lass,' said Marion. 'We just came to 'elp 'em find thee. We'll be wi't rest of marchers now.'

Ellie looked relieved. 'Well then, welcome to Tinkers' cave then. Come an' 'ave a look.'

Saying this, she took Ruth by the hand and led the party round the corner from where the light was glowing. They moved into a spacious cavern about twelve feet high and twenty feet across, with three wooden barrels each about four feet high and what looked like a caldron against the back wall. There were several stacks of smaller kegs piled up against the walls. The cavern was dimly lit by ten candles set at different points. Short steps were pushed against the barrels, and a ladle lay on the top rung. Sacks, some full and some half empty, lay against the wall of the cave. There was a sound of running water coming from beyond the chamber.

'This is it,' Ellie said proudly. 'This is where we make th'ale. Me dad's out now; he tries to give me orders every day, though truth to tell, 'e's usually out. So it's me what spends day firing up charcoal for t'caldron to get malt from barley, boiling it with 'ops, adding in t'yeast and running wi' pails of water from t'spring to t'barrels. So I could do wi' a bit of 'elp. That way, tha' can pay for tha' lodging,' she said, smiling. 'An' lodging'll be round 'ere.'

Ellie picked a candle from a ledge on the cave wall and beckoned them to follow her. She went round a corner into a deeper recess of the cave, where there were two straw pallets lying on the floor.

'We'll get another o' these easily enough,' she said.

The children were delighted to have the security of such a well-hidden retreat. Marion sensed that it would be cold and damp, but could see that they were not likely to find a better hiding place.

'Well, tha'll be alreet 'ere,' she said. 'Ellie, will your dad be 'appy wi' this? Can we talk to 'im?'

'I'd not know where 'e is, me duck.' said Ellie. 'I 'aven't seen 'im since 'e dragged me away from your campfire last night. But, don't worry, 'e'll be right enough. 'E's no friend o' magistrates,' she smiled.

Marion looked at Ruth and Joshua with a question in her eyes. Would they be happy to take Ellie's word for it? Ruth understood the question and nodded her head to Marion.

'Well, Jim an' I will leave thee now. But we'll be back tomorrow in t'morning wi' whatever news of your dad and t'others we've got.'

'Won't tha' 'ave a glass of Tinkers' best afore tha' goes?' asked Ellie.

'I'll not say no to that,' said Jim.

'Nor me,' said Marion.

Ellie reached deep into one of the barrels with her ladle and filled two glass mugs to the brim, passing them with foam running over the top to Marion and Jim.

'This is a fine Nottingham breakfast, lass,' said Jim.

'Aye, 'n' if me dad were 'ere, it'd cost you a penny,' said Ellie. 'But I'll let you off.'

'Best drink up then, Jim,' said Marion, 'or thou'll be in t'gaol too, for I know tha' 'asn't a farthing, never mind a penny.'

They downed their glasses, and Marion hugged both the children before leaving.

'Look after yourselves. We'll be 'ere tomorrow, about this time.'

Ellie kept Ruth and Joshua busy all that day. Not only did they have to draw beer out of the barrels into smaller kegs, but also to keep ladling the barley and malt into the caldron and occasionally shovelling charcoal beneath it. Ellie moved to and fro, giving a series of orders. At about midday, she had decided they needed additional supplies of charcoal and suggested she leave them for a short time as she begged and borrowed from neighbours. Ruth and Joshua had looked nervous and eventually they had all agreed they should move together.

Ellie took them on a quick tour of the brewers of Castle Hill, with all of whom she seemed to be on the best of terms. Ruth and Joshua could see that exchanging and borrowing supplies, with no money passing hands, was the normal practice in this community.

They found children working in most of the caves, many of whom looked tired and dispirited, but who managed a smile for Ellie, whose home was apparently a meeting place most evenings.

'See tha' to-neet, then,' said Ellie to a girl in the last brewing shop they visited. ''Ave got these 'ere visitors that'll fair fleece tha' at dominoes.'

As they left, she explained to Ruth and Joshua that the children met to play dominoes most nights, gambling with lace makers' needles – a common commodity in Nottingham with a value of two for a farthing.

'But I never get more 'n six 'n' lose 'em all by t'end of t'game,' she said laughingly.

The brewing kept them busy for the rest of the day. By six o'clock, six of the children they had spoken with in the morning had assembled in the cave for the game. Ruth and Joshua could see this was a well-established routine, as Mick, the smallest of the visitors, produced a bag of dominoes. With a knowledgeable look on his face,

With Ellie in the Nottingham caves

Mick distributed the pieces to each of the nine players, as Ruth and Joshua had been added to the group. He then produced a stack of a dozen lace makers' needles and laid them down by his side; Ellie led the play and the others followed her lead. Much to his surprise, and Mick's dismay, Joshua won the first round and was awarded the first of the lace needles.

Just as Mick was picking up the dominoes from the other children, Ellie's father, Davy, burst into the room.

'An' what are you lot doing 'ere?' he cried.

'Dad, tha' knows they come 'ere every day,' said Ellie. 'There's nowt new.'

Davy looked at the group, slightly swaying on his feet.

'Oh yes, there is,' he said. 'Them two. Who are they?'

'They're children o' thy friends t'Chartists,' said Ellie.

'An' I've invited 'em to stay wi'us,' she added defiantly.

Davy looked suspicious. In the course of that day, he'd seen all his work of organising the Chartists in Nottingham collapse as the soldiers had arrested the ringleaders. In fear for their own safety, the Nottingham leaders had split up, and Davy had spent the day below ground in the cave-like cellar of The Bell Inn, where the cellar keeper who drew ale from the wooden casks had given him a tankard which had seldom been empty.

The drink made a bad situation seem all the more desperate to him. He had been in gaol before for two years for being part of the mob that ransacked the castle when it had been burned down six years earlier, and the prospect of going back to gaol frightened him. At that time, he'd been together with Ellie's mother who had been reduced to begging in the streets of the city using her pretty six-year-old daughter to attract sympathy.

'Well, tha' can get tha' friends out of 'ere this minute,' said Davy, looking angrily at the group of children still seated in a circle round the dominoes.

'Ruth and Joshua, get t'back cave where them beds are,' said Ellie. 'The rest of you'd best be gone. Tha' knows what me dad can do when 'e's like this.'

Mick and his friends were used to Davy's angry moods and had to abandon their game at least once a fortnight. They made for the cave door, scuttling past Davy as he continued to stare angrily at Ellie.

'So tha' thinks to defy me, lass, then?' he said.

Ellie was watching her father's hands and judging the distance to a leather strap which hung on the wall. It was in these moods that he would use it to beat her, but for the time being, he continued to sway uncertainly on the spot.

'I'm not saying owt to thee, Dad,' she said. 'I'm just giving shelter to the children of thy friends. Don't you realise they've walked 'ere? Walked for miles and miles, over t'moors from some faraway town wi' a name like

Todmortown or summut. They're tired and 'ungry and their dad, one o' your Chartist friends who's brought them on this march, is in gaol as far as we can make out.'

Davy softened at this cry from the heart as it reached his muddled brain. Fighting for time, he said, 'But 'ow long'll they stay for?'

''Appen till 'e gets out,' Ellie said, unsure of her answer and remembering Davy's own two years in gaol.

'That could be a very long time… as tha' knows, Ellie,' he added.

'Well, we're not planning the next five years, Dad,' said Ellie. 'We're planning tomorrow. No more.'

'Well, lass,' he said, 'maybe just the two of 'em. And till tomorrow night then.' Ellie smiled quickly. She would worry about the next day when it came.

Ruth and Joshua had been tense and wary, listening to this conversation from the inner cave. Davy's manner seemed dangerous enough to suggest they might find themselves thrown out of the cave into the cold night, uncertain how to find Marion and Jim and the rest of the marchers. But when Ellie came round the corner, she was beaming.

'Well, you 'eard that, me ducks. Tha' can stay. Ruth an' me'll sleep on that pallet an' I'll be getting another from Mick's.'

'That's grand, Ellie,' said Ruth.

'I knew you'd save us,' said Joshua.

'Well, gaol's no good for children like us now, is it?' said Ellie. 'We'll leave that to them adults.'

Marion's suspicion that the cave would be cold and damp proved to be unfounded. The walls of the cave were remarkably dry; and Ruth and Joshua, exhausted from lack of sleep the previous night and the excitement of the arrests, slept well on the pallets. Only Davy tossed and turned as he struggled with his hangover from drinking too much and his depression at the collapse of the Chartist stand in Nottingham.

It was Marion's voice at the entry to the cave that woke and roused the children.

'Ellie, Ruth, Joshua; I'm coming in. It's me 'n' Jim,' she said.

'Marion, Jim. Come in,' cried Ruth, getting up and rushing through the cave to the outer door.

As Marion came through the canvas flap, Ruth rushed into her arms, saying: 'As t'got news o' Dad?'

'I 'ave, lass; and it's none so good' Marion said despondently.

'Will they 'ang 'im?' said Joshua, as he and Ellie joined them.

'No, we reckon they'll not go that far,' said Jim. 'All we know so far is that your Dad and t'others were charged at t'county court yesterday wi' what they call

'Conspiring to Create a Disturbance'. They've been sent to gaol until they can bring 'em to trial.'

'An' when'll that be?' asked Ruth.

At that moment Davy, more dishevelled than ever, walked into the outer cave.

''Appen one month, 'appen six month,' he said. 'Wi' me, it were five month waiting wi' rats, then into courtroom, then back wi' t'rats for another two year. An' I never saw you, Ellie, all that time, did I now?'

'No, Dad, that's reet,' said Ellie, deciding that she could afford to humour her father this morning. 'But it'll 'appen be quicker for Ruth and Joshua's dad.'

'An' 'appen it won't,' said Davy.

'Marion, I must see 'im,' said Ruth. 'Now. Today. I can't wait six months; I can't wait a day.'

She turned to Joshua.

'Joshua, a'ta coming? At least we can look at prison where they've got 'im chained up like as not.'

Joshua was not so sure.

'What if they tak us in too, Ruth? Dad wouldn't want that,' he said.

'No, 'e would not,' said Marion. 'An' I'm going to make sure they don't get a chance.'

'Well, we can just go and look at walls o' prison,' said Ruth. 'An' think on where 'e is.'

Ellie had been listening carefully and realised how much Ruth wanted to feel near to her father.

'What if we three go together?' she said. 'They'll never recognise just the three of us children.'

'Ellie, would you come wi'us? That'd be grand,' said Ruth.

'They'd best go, Marion,' said Jim. 'If they stay cooped up 'ere, they'll go mad by th'end o' day.'

Marion could see the sense of this but was worried that they would try to talk their way into the prison.

'Well, you three go then,' she said. 'But come straight back. Me and Jim'll wait for thee 'ere for about two hour, and then we'll come looking.'

Ruth gave Marion a hug and led the other two out of the cave. 'Look after Marion and Jim, Dad. They'll need a bit o'breakfast. Fancy some ale, Jim?' cried Ellie with a laugh as she left the cave.

Ellie led the way into the maze of streets through which Ruth and Joshua had passed.

'It's market day today,' said Ellie. 'They come from miles around wi' owt to sell. Look at them 'ens.'

As she spoke, Ellie was nearly knocked over by two big men carrying a pole between them, across which was strung a pannier basket packed with live hens. Soon they caught up with a boy of about their own age with a stick slung across his shoulders pierced with dried fish. Close by him was a girl struggling with two pails of large mushrooms.

'Tha'll see this lot and much more up for sale in a few minutes,' said Ellie.

But Ruth and Joshua, who would normally have been fascinated by the bustling scene, felt even more depressed by the energetic life around them.

'Let's just get on, Ellie,' said Ruth. 'We'll not stop for t'market today.'

But as the children came into Exchange Square, they could not help being overwhelmed by the bustle and excitement of the scene. Although it was still only just after eight o'clock, a good hundred stallholders had laid out their wares. At the opposite end of the square was a theatre with a banner spread across it, announcing the latest production: *The True Story of Queen Caroline.* Walking in its direction, the children passed cobblers repairing boots on the spot, knife-grinders offering to sharpen any blade a housewife or kitchen servant could produce, rows of bonneted countrywomen selling milk, eggs and cheese, fishmongers with their fresh fish scattered amongst ice blocks, dried fish being sold from sticks and a range of textile goods. Joshua saw wool, silk and cotton all on separate stalls and closest to the theatre, stands of Nottingham hosiery and lace.

For a moment, Ruth and Joshua stood still with eyes wide open. Ellie looked at them in turn.

'Yes, that's Nottingham market for you,' she said. 'I bet Mick's out there somewhere. This is 'is gang's best patch. They can get through more pockets on a market day than any other.'

'What, you mean Mick's a pickpocket?' said Ruth.

'Aye, an' a right good one,' said Ellie, amused at Ruth's innocence. 'In fact, that's where 'e gets 'is lace needles,' she said, pointing to the stalls where hand tools for lacemaking were being sold. 'That is, when they're not looking.'

The news of Mick's real occupation jolted Ruth and Joshua back to thoughts of prison.

'Come on, let's be off,' said Ruth.

They passed down the side of the theatre, soon passing the old church of St Peter's, through another maze of streets and into a broader street which again seemed to be packed with people. They were a strange mixture of the smart and the dishevelled – men with top hats and ladies in billowing dresses, cavalry officers on horseback in red and white uniforms, working men wearing rough calico shirts and clogs, women with shawls and bonnets, and children dressed in rags running barefoot. As Joshua followed Ruth and Ellie through the crowd, he wondered if he would see Mick with his hand in the pocket of a gentleman or the shopping basket of a lady.

But it was not long before the three children found themselves at the back of a crowd gathered outside iron railings set in front of a tall, imposing building. Looking up above the heads of those in front of them, they could see the tops of four great columns supporting an overhanging square parapet.

'That's it,' said Ellie. 'That's t'court'ouse, an' prison's just behind. They 'ang folk just in front o' them railings. Tha' dad'll be somewhere in t'prison behind.'

Ruth had not quite abandoned the idea of trying to see her father. She really believed that once she and Joshua told the prison officers who they were they would not simply let her visit and leave. However, her heart fell as she saw the impossibility of getting through the crowd, finding somebody to take them seriously and getting in and out of the prison in safety.

'Let's get t'front,' said Ellie, pushing her way between the hundred or more people gathered in front of the railings. As Ruth and Joshua followed her, they began to recognise some of the men who had been on the march with them.

As they reached the front of the crowd, Joshua was delighted to see Jethro leaning on his crutch, examining the flow of people passing through the large doorway of the courthouse.

'Well, Joshua, lad. I'll be damned. 'Ere you are, lad, an' tha' sister too.' Leaning down to their height, he said more softly: 'But I thought you two were in 'iding wi' this lass.'

'Well, we are,' said Joshua, 'but we 'eard that Dad was 'ere and just wanted to see the place.'

'Do you think they'd let us in to see 'im, Jethro?' said Ruth.

'Now then, lass, don't set your mind on that. Tha'
'eard what that man from t'newspapers, Steele, 'ad to
say. They might clap thee inside wi' tha' dad.

He pointed over to the other side of the crowd where
William Steele was easily distinguished by his green suit
and grey top hat. He too noticed the children as Jethro
bent down to speak to them, and quickly came over.

'What are you two doing here? I thought you were
safe in a cave with your friend Ellie. Why, that must be
you!' he said, looking at Ellie's dirty face and golden locks.

'Aye, that's me,' said Ellie. 'An' these two are safe
enough wi'me.'

'But we 'ad to come 'ere, Mr Steele,' said Ruth.
'Soon as Marion told us that Dad's in prison 'ere, we
'ad to come.'

'Well, I can see that you wanted to, but I'd advise
you to leave right away. There are police and informers
all about. And your friend Ralph Murphy's not far
away. I saw him this morning in this very street.'

At this, Ruth and Joshua recognised the danger
they were in and looked at each other.

'Ruth, we'd best be off wi' Ellie,' said Joshua.

'Aye, tha's right enough,' said Ruth wearily.

'That will be best,' said Steele. 'But there's some
hope. The magistrates had no right to charge your father
and the others. If they really had created a disturbance,
that's one thing, but planning a peaceful meeting is
another. I've reported all this in *The Times*, and I believe

they'll make it the main article. With luck, it will be in the newspaper today. It should have an effect on the government. Lie low with Ellie and I'll keep in touch with you through Marion.'

'You'd best come, lass,' said Ellie, who sensed how reluctant Ruth was to move from the spot.

'We'll wait for the news from Marion then,' said Ruth quietly and turned to go back through the crowd.

'Bye, Jethro,' said Joshua, looking up at the old soldier.

'Look after tha'self, lad,' said Jethro. 'We'll be watching to make sure they don't move your dad and t'others somewhere else. Be careful now.'

The children threaded their way back through the busy streets, this time avoiding the market and taking Castlegate which brought them under the castle hill in about a quarter of an hour. They immediately found themselves opposite an army barracks built up against the castle rock, outside of which about fifty infantrymen were drilling. Joshua recognised the uniforms of the soldiers who had arrested his father and the other leaders. He suddenly stopped, while walking alongside Ellie and Ruth, and stood in shock, fearful that the soldiers would march over and arrest all three of them.

'What's wrong with thee, Joshua?' cried Ellie. 'Hasn't you seen soldiers afore?'

'But these are the ones that arrested Dad and cut down Jethro,' said Joshua.

'Aye, they would be,' said Ellie. 'But they live 'ere, just round from t'caves and tha'd best get used to 'em. They're t'Robin Hood Rifles an' some of 'em come for a keg of ale every day. I don't know 'ow they get through it. Now come on, you're supposed to be in 'iding. Let's get back t'cave.'

Joshua relaxed as he saw the soldiers continue with their drilling and realised they could walk unscathed along the side of the castle rock down towards the caves. As Ellie pushed aside the flap, she found her father, Jim and Marion engaged in a deep discussion. Davy and Jim each had a tankard in front of them. Marion was sitting slightly apart, watching the two men drink their ale. They all looked up as the flap was pushed back and the other two children followed her into the cave. Marion's face lit up with relief and delight as she saw that Ruth and Joshua had arrived back safely.

'What, not in gaol?' she said laughingly. 'I'm right glad to see thee, Ruth and Joshua. I dinn'a fancy visiting you in gaol.'

'An' like as not never coming out thyself, lass,' said Jim to Marion.

'Ellie, tha's done well, lass,' said Davy. 'Are there many folk at t'court'ouse?'

'Aye, street's right full. There's soldiers, beggars and grand folk so tha' can hardly move. But some of Ruth and Joshua's friends were there. One grand bloke in a top 'at, like of which I'd never spoken to before, an' what said 'e worked for a newspaper, told 'em they'd better stay with us in 'iding.'

'An' what's folks' mood?' asked Davy.

'Well, I'd say it's as if they're waiting for summut but don't know what,' said Ellie.

''Appen I should get down there and speak to 'em,' said Davy, looking into his tankard.

'Dad, tha'd best stay 'ere too,' said Ellie, knowing only too well that a tankard of ale could move her father from fear to a foolhardy boldness in less than half an hour.

'There were a good number of cavalry men there,' added Ruth, who could see that Ellie was now concerned for her father.

'Well then, Ellie,' said Davy, 'we'll 'ave a working day 'ere and tha' can keep me and tha' friends out of prison.'

'An' we'd best get back t'field where rest o' march is,' said Marion. 'There were a few slipping away this morning, and we don't need to add t'numbers. We'll be back tomorrow, you two.'

As Marion and Jim walked across to the door, Ellie again became the efficient manager of the brewery. She calculated that the best way to take the minds of Ruth and Joshua off their predicament was to put them to work. Davy was only too delighted to watch the brewing from a stool, and his attitude to Ruth and Joshua had softened to one of welcome by the middle of the day. In turn, although neither of the children forgot their danger, they were happy enough to work with Ellie. At the end of the day, when Mick and his friends came round for a game of dominoes, Davy quietly left the cave to the children. This time, Ruth and Joshua stood in some awe of Mick as a champion pickpocket and were happy enough to see him sweep up all the lace needles.

When he awoke the next morning, Joshua felt the cold seeping into every part of his body. Even Ellie, hardened as she was to living in the cave, felt the chill going through her and sensed that these were the first signs of winter. Her memory of the two winters she had barely survived while her father was in gaol made her particularly gloomy at its approach.

Joshua pulled the coat which his mother had made closer about him.

'Ellie, I'll never survive this,' he said.

'An' I thought you were the 'eroes of a great moorland march,' said Ellie. 'Weren't it cold on them tops?'

'Cold enough, but we kept moving,' said Ruth. 'And anyway, we 'ad shelter each night. An' not in a cave,' she added crossly.

'Well, that's some kind of thanks,' said Ellie, lying next to Ruth on their pallet and looking at the roof of the cave above them.

Ruth realised that she had spoken carelessly.

'Nay, Ellie, I didn'a mean that,' she said. 'We know what we owe you.'

'Well, I'll 'ave a stay with thee in Todmortown or whatever it is, one of these days,' said Ellie.

'Todmortown! What's this Todmortown I'm 'earing?' came a musical voice from the outer cave. 'Tha' means Todmorden,' said Marion as she burst through into the area where the children were sleeping.

'An' one Todmorden man's going to be released from jail today,' she added with delight. 'Look 'ere, it's in this paper.' Marion, closely followed by Jim, was carrying a copy of a folded newspaper and waving with her right hand.

'Tha' mean Dad's going to be freed!' said Ruth. 'Can it be true, Marion?'

'Well, it says it 'ere clear enough,' said Marion, spreading out the paper on a broad shelf of rock. As she unfolded the paper, all that the children could see on the front page was *THE TIMES* in large print, followed by a mass of advertisements.

''Ow can tha' make owt o' that?' said Ruth, who had never tried to read a newspaper before.

'No, it's inside, lass,' said Marion, turning to the centre page where large print spread across a single column headlined the news. Ruth and Joshua looked at the page, but neither of them could read properly. Marion had been taught to read at Sunday School. 'I'm not right good at reading, but I'll 'ave a go at this. Just listen.'

CHARTIST ARREST IN NOTTINGHAM
HOME SECRETARY ORDERS RELEASE

Nottingham, Wednesday evening. Our report of Tuesday confirmed the arrest of five of the leaders of the Chartist march, now bringing the Charter with a reported one million signatures to Parliament in London. The five leaders were Mr Feargus O'Connor, Mr Francis Place, Mr Ben Mather, Mr Frank Sykes and Mr Jess Midgeley. They were arrested by a column of the Robin Hood Rifles on the instructions of the magistrate Sir Henry Fowler and were charged with conspiring to disrupt the peace. They were then committed to gaol pending trial which the magistrate stated would take place 'after some months'.

The right of the magistrates to disrupt a peaceful demonstration in support of the Charter was raised in the House of Commons yesterday by John Fielden, the Radical member for Oldham. He called on the Prime Minister, Lord Melbourne, to instruct the Lord Lieutenant of Nottinghamshire to release the Chartist leaders forthwith since they never had the intention of disrupting the peace. Mr Fielden had the support not only of his fellow Radical Thomas Attwood (Member for Birmingham) but also of a large number of members of the Whig Party. The Prime Minister sensed the mood of members and agreed to instruct the Lord Lieutenant to release the Chartist leaders on bail. The Home Secretary would review the question of whether charges against the five men should later be dropped.

Mr Fielden pressed for confirmation of the date by which the men would be released and was informed that the Lord Lieutenant would be asked to release them by noon on Thursday.

Our correspondent will continue to report from Nottingham.

Ruth and Joshua looked at Marion in wonder. 'So Dad will really be out then?' said Ruth.

'I reckon we can thank Mr Steele for this,' said Joshua.

'Aye, 'e looked right enough. Didn't I tell you, Dad?' said Ellie as her father joined the group.

Davy's face began to light up as he heard the news. He looked and felt like a man reprieved from a gaol sentence himself.

'Aye, we'd best see if we can find 'im and thank 'im. 'E'll be down at Shire Hall soon, like as not,' said Davy. 'An' that's where we've got to be to give them lads a grand welcome when they come out. But I'd best get to John Wilson's 'ouse to make sure we get a big crowd on t'streets by noon. Tha' go down wi' tha' friends, Ellie.'

'Nowt'll keep me away from that, Dad,' said Ellie. 'We'd best go now.'

'Aye, before they change their mind,' said Marion, folding up the newspaper. As she did so, Ruth and Joshua both folded their arms round her waist, saying nothing, but loving her all the more for bringing the good news.

Although it was still only nine o'clock, the children could not wait to position themselves outside Shire Hall. As they threaded their way back through the streets, they found they were part of a surge of people moving in the same direction. News of the promised release of the Chartists' leaders had already swept through the city. Many of those who had planned to attend the meeting, which was cancelled now, wished to welcome the leaders back into freedom.

While two days earlier, as the children walked down High Pavement to Shire Hall, the crowd had included all kinds of people – smart and dishevelled, army officers and working men – it was now almost all working men and women. There was a sea of jubilant but grimy faces on all sides, many of whom had left their work as a group as the news had spread. Ellie, Ruth and Joshua found themselves overshadowed by this mass of adults with no children in sight. Suddenly they caught sight of a figure of about their height walking a few yards in front of them, wearing a black cap tilted at a slight angle.

'Isn't that Mick wi' that cap?' said Ruth.

'Aye, we couldn't mistake that now, could we?' said Ellie. 'Eyup, Mick, come on 'ere!'

The peaked cap was reversed to reveal Mick's smiling face, as he stopped to let them draw level with him.

'Well, me ducks, tha's swept the needles up this time right enough,' said Mick.

'An' what brings you 'ere?' said Ellie.

'Well, not the pockets of this lot anyway,' said Mick, smiling and waving his hand at the crowd. Lowering his voice, he added:

'I'll bet there's not a leather purse or a snuff box between 'em. No, tha' knows me, Ellie. If there's summut going on in Nottingham, Mick likes to be there.'

'Well, there'll be summut today right enough,' said Ruth. 'It's not every day we get our dad out o'gaol!'

Her relief at the prospect of the release was catching. As they walked the last quarter of a mile to Shire Hall, Ruth and Joshua felt more light-hearted than at any time since they had left Todmorden. Joshua quickly spotted Jethro at the end of the railings closest to the main door and led the others towards him.

'Joshua and Ruth, a great good morning to tha', and to tha' friends. This is grand news and better than I ever expected to 'ave. Probably the best since they locked up Boney on St 'Elena.'

'Does't a think they'll really let dad out, Jethro?' said

Joshua, who suddenly began to wonder if his father really would emerge at noon.

'Aye, lad, that I do. For if 'e an t'others don't appear, these railings'll be torn apart, and I wouldn't wonder if we won't find a Samson to pull them pillars down. An' then this Shire 'All and court'ouse would go wi'em and I wouldn't wonder if the 'ole of Nottingham wouldn't follow soon after.'

Joshua enjoyed the idea of Nottingham being pulled apart to get his father out of gaol and was relieved by Jethro's words. In any case, it was difficult not to be carried along by the mood of the crowd which was hopeful and expectant. Jethro was now organising a 'guard of honour', as he called it, to provide a line on either side of the Shire Hall door through which the leaders were expected to be released. The guard numbered about twenty of the marchers who had been camping in the meadow and, since Jethro was organising it, included both Jim Knotts and Judd Ackroyd, who was carrying his sledgehammer with the head hanging over his shoulder as if it were a billhook. The guard had cut rough staves from trees close to the meadow where they had camped and now prepared to form an arch with these as the leaders were released into the street.

It was now eleven thirty, and the atmosphere of exuberance was turning to tension as noon approached. Ruth spotted the grey top hat of William Steele close to the railings on the other side of the guard. It was easy to see amidst a sea of caps, for most of the top-hatted folk of two days ago had disappeared. She felt a surge of gratitude to this tall man who was so polite but whose writing seemed to have persuaded even Parliament that her father and the others should be freed. As soon as she saw him, she dashed through the lines of the guard and coming out the other side, cried with a beaming face:

'Mr Steele, Mr Steele; it's right good to see tha'. What tha's done is just wonderful. We were near dead wi' fear. I can't believe it.'

'Well, I did say you should have some hope two days ago, didn't I? *The Times* isn't any old newspaper, you know, but then your friend Mr Fielden isn't any old Member of Parliament. You should be thanking him as well, but don't worry; I'll send him your thanks in advance. Anyway, we haven't seen them come out yet. Let's not count our chickens before they're hatched.'

By this time, the other three children had twisted their way through the legs and waists of the guard and were standing close to William Steele, admiring him from three feet away. Suddenly a roar broke out from the crowd, and they all turned towards the door of Shire Hall to see the great frame of Feargus O'Connor march out into the daylight. He was closely followed by Francis Place, Ben Mather, Frank Sykes and Jess Midgeley. The magistrates had followed their instructions to the letter.

As O'Connor came out, he paused and seemed to hesitate as to whether to open his mouth. As he hesitated, Ellie saw her father dash up the steps of the hall and speak into O'Connor's ear. O'Connor nodded to him, and Davy, who had now recovered his confidence, shouted to the crowd:

'Mr O'Connor'll speak in Exchange Square as soon as he can get there. Make way there.'

Immediately after Davy spoke, the five leaders walked briskly under the arch made by the guard of honour as the crowd threw their caps in the air and cheers rose on all sides. The children had watched with delight as their father emerged with the other leaders, only to feel dismay as they saw them immediately hoisted onto the shoulders of the last five of the guards. William Steele realised their disappointment but also saw that they had no chance of catching up with Jess as he was carried along by the guards in the midst of the seething crowd.

'I'm afraid you'll not get to him now,' he said. 'He won't even be able to hear you in the midst of this. You'd best follow them to the market square. Let's go together.'

Ruth managed to swallow her disappointment, but Joshua could hardly hold back tears of frustration. The last three days had been difficult to bear, and now there were thousands of people separating him from his father. Seeing his anguish, Ellie said quietly:

'Cheer up, lad; it'll not be long now. Just a bit more o' that patience tha's 'ad just to get 'ere.'

She took his hand as the children were again swept up in the mass of people on the way to the market. After ten minutes of struggling through the streets,

Jess is released from Nottingham Prison

they found the crowd begin to thin out as it spilled into the square. A hundred yards ahead, they could see the leaders, still being carried shoulder-high, nearing the theatre at the side of the square. A makeshift platform of market stalls had been arranged and the guards were carrying them towards this. Within another five minutes, the leaders were on the platform, and John Wilson, the Nottingham leader, was trying to appeal for quiet so that Feargus O'Connor could speak. But only O'Connor's voice was strong enough to begin to quell the noise from the crowd. Jess Midgeley stood alongside the others, looking uncomfortable with his prominent position, his eyes beginning to search the crowd.

By this time, the children had managed to push their way to the front and were only a few yards from their father. As he saw them, he waved his right hand with joy and beckoned them to come round the back of the platform. Ellie and Mick held back as Ruth and Joshua went round to the back where a ladder was placed, and climbed up to Jess. Stepping from the ladder to the platform, they were delighted to be with him again, whether alone or in front of a crowd over three thousand strong.

'Dad, we thought we'd never see you again,' said Joshua.

'And you'd be chained up in Nottingham Gaol forever,' said Ruth.

'Well, I wasn't so sure myself,' said Jess, 'but here we are in broad daylight and the two of you still smiling.'

'I wish mam could see us now,' said Ruth.

'Well, I'm not right sure that she'd be too 'appy,' said Jess. 'She never did like anything public.' And he hugged them close to him.

By this time, O'Connor had managed to quieten the crowd.

'Well, we're finally out, my lads. I won't call it justice, but I will call it good news. Good news for the Charter, good news for all working men and women, and good news for the children whose lives are made a misery by working from first light to last light. And we've got two of them here. What's more, they've marched with us over a hundred mile including over some of the roughest moorland in England. And now they'll be marching with us to London and Parliament.'

At this, the crowd renewed its cheering, and hundreds of caps were thrown into the air.

'There's a good two thousand have marched with us from Manchester and have camped in the field by the River Trent here. And we're well on to getting a million signatures for the Charter. Let's have a good twenty thousand more before we leave Nottingham. Mr John Wilson here has arranged for the signature scrolls to be laid out here as soon as me and my fellow gaolbirds go back to our camp.

'And let's have a good thousand of you lads join us for the rest of the march to London. You'll be there in a week, and back in another, and three thousand marchers in Parliament Square'll be no joke, I can tell you, for we'll get the London lads out too and fill the place till it's fit to burst.'

Ruth had been too bound up in her reunion with her father to listen to the first part of O'Connor's speech. As she began to hear what he was saying, she wondered why he was always talking about 'lads'. Hadn't he noticed that she and Marion were women? Or that a good third of the crowd in front of them were also women? She would talk to Marion about it later – it seemed scant recognition for their efforts on the march so far, or for her mother's decision to let Joshua and her join the march. She listened again to what O'Connor was saying.

He spoke for another ten minutes in a similar vein and was followed by John Wilson who spoke for the Nottingham Chartists. He finished by saying:

'Those of you who are fit and free to march to London should be over at the camp by t'River Trent at seven tomorrow morning, and for those of you who can't come – we'll tak your signatures with us. And thanks to all of you who gave porridge and oatcakes to keep these brave marchers alive.'

Ruth and Joshua were glad to be the first off the platform. Ellie and Mick were waiting for them at the bottom of the makeshift steps.

'Well, me ducks,' said Ellie, 'tha'll be off to London?'

'Some pockets ripe for picking there, I 'ear,' said Mick.

'Why don't you come wi' us?' said Ruth, hoping that Ellie would come and Mick would stay.

'Nay, lass, that's not for me,' said Ellie. 'I'm sure me dad'll want to join thee. 'E never could resist the idea o' London – though 'e's never been there. Somebody's got to keep brewing t'beer and a few pence coming in, and that'll be me. An' as for Mick – tha'd never want 'im wi' thee in London. Tha'd be in jail thaself inside a day.'

'Then we'll not see either of you again. Once we get back to Todmorden, tha'll not see us south again,' said Joshua.

'No, but that's where I'm coming to see thee, lad,' said Ellie. 'I can't miss visiting a place wi' a name like that. You tell me they'll 'ave a railway there afore long, an' they say we'll 'ave one 'ere too – an' so I'll save me pennies an' come an' visit thee when they're done.'

Ruth understood Ellie well enough to know that Ellie herself had no idea if she really would try to visit them by train, or any other means. But she wanted to tell them she would be thinking of them and would miss them. Ruth felt the tears welling up in her eyes: she would miss this free spirit who was so different to herself, but so warm. For once speechless, she clasped Ellie round the neck and let her tears flow into her friend's messy golden hair. Joshua and Mick stood their distance, wishing they could let their tears flow too.

Suddenly Jess and Davy appeared at their side.

'Ruth,' said Jess, 'are you ready now, lass?'

'Yes,' said Ruth hesitantly, 'I think I am, Dad,' as she pulled herself away from Ellie.

Managing to remember that her father had never met Ellie, she added: 'An' this is Ellie what 'id us and kept us from being takken to join you.'

'An' that's me dad,' added Ellie, pointing at Davy.

Jess and Davy looked at each other warily before breaking into smiles and shaking hands.

'You'll come and see us, Ellie?' said Ruth.

'Aye, tha' can be sure o' that, me duck,' said Ellie. 'Are you going wi'em to London, Dad?'

Davy looked at his feet. 'Well, love, if you'll mind shop for a couple o' weeks, we'll 'ave Charter presented an' I'll be back in no time.'

Ellie looked at Mick. 'Right, Mick, we've got work to do. Let's be off and let these travellers get on their way.' With a wave of her hand, she disappeared into the crowd, with Mick following behind her. Ruth and Joshua looked up at their dad, and Joshua said quietly:

'Let's go back to the camping field, Dad.'

'Aye, right enough, lad,' said Jess as the four of them walked with the rest of the marchers out of the square.

CHAPTER 8

LONDON AT LAST

Sometimes the road was separated from the fields by a hedge; sometimes the grass ran right up to the road. Every quarter of an hour or so, a stagecoach carrying a good fifteen people, inside and out, struggled with the column of marchers for a portion of the road. The drivers seemed to take a particular delight in spattering the column with small stones and mud as their teams of eight horses were driven as close as possible to the marchers. Ruth was walking on the outside of a row, which included Marion and Jim, and as she looked up at the giant swaying coaches, she could see both fear and hatred written on the faces of the passengers perched on the top of the coach.

'Look at 'em. Should be locked up, the lot of 'em,' said one middle-aged man in a battered grey top hat.

'And dragging their wretched children with them!' said a lady sitting beside him, who looked as if she felt she should be inside the coach.

'Wretched yourself!' shouted Joshua in reply, just in time to get an apple core thrown at him as the coach raced on towards the head of the column.

Both Ruth and Joshua had been expecting that somehow their welcome would grow warmer as they came closer to London. They could not help feeling that these brushes with the stagecoaches were a bad omen, for the word being passed down the column was that London was now very close.

In fact, they saw little change in the countryside for another mile or so: there were green fields on each side of them. But eventually they sensed that the rows ahead of them were marching faster. Marion was the first in the group closest to Ruth and Joshua to realise the meaning of the faster pace.

'This'll be it then, you two,' she said. 'We must be getting really close now. An' I don't know about you, but I can scarce walk another yard.'

'Marion, I never expected to 'ear tha' say that,' said Ruth.

'Well, tha's 'eard right enough, lass,' said Marion. 'I can't wait till we've given in t'Charter and got back on't road to Tod.'

'Nay, lass,' said Jim. 'What about Queen and Tower o' London. Surely tha' wants to see them before tha' gets back to 'Eathcote's sewing shop?'

''Eathcote'll not 'ave me back after this lot,' said Marion. 'An' a'm not so sure about t'Queen. They say she gets fifty thousand pounds a year. There are a few childer I know what could use some o' that. I'll not be 'olding back for staring at 'er.'

'Well, whatever there is to see, we'll see it soon,' said Jim, as they felt the road beginning a gradual descent.

Looking ahead, they could see that the column had begun to lose its formation and was spilling out into a disorganised crowd. As the rows around them merged into the crowd, Ruth and Joshua struggled for a place at the front. As they emerged, they could see green fields stretching before them but beyond the fields and still distant, what looked like a model of a city.

'That must be it,' said Joshua. 'But it looks right small from 'ere.'

'Aye, but big enough when yer inside it, lad,' said a big man behind him with a gruff voice. 'D'yer see that building wiv a round top, li'e a dome? That's St Paul's Cathedral and it's the biggest in t'world. It'd take more than a thousand of you, piled one on top of the other, to get t'top.'

'St Paul's?' said Ruth. 'Oh, aye, I've 'eard o' that in Sunday School. Christopher Wren what built it, weren't it, and used to be 'auled up in a weft box to see 'ow they were getting on wi' roof?'

'Well, you know a thing, to be sure,' said the big man behind her with what Ruth guessed was a cockney accent. 'But you can only see what they call the City from 'ere. That's all the banks what've got our money.

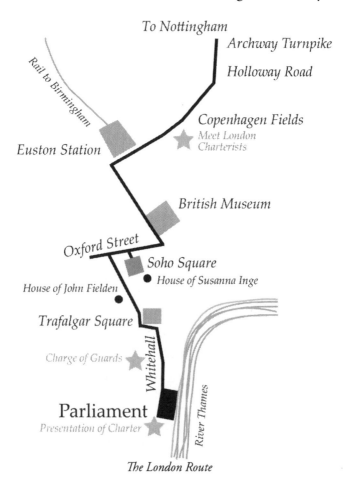

To Nottingham

Archway Turnpike

Holloway Road

Rail to Birmingham

Copenhagen Fields
Meet London
Charterists

Euston Station

British Museum

Oxford Street

Soho Square

House of John Fielden

House of Susanna Inge

Trafalgar Square

Whitehall

Charge of Guards

Parliament
Presentation of Charter

River Thames

The London Route

Parliament and Buckingham Palace are away to the right and you can't see them from 'ere.'

'It still looks a long way,' said Joshua.

'We'll be there soon enough now,' said the big man. 'This is the Archway Turnpike, an' once we're through it, we'll be along 'olloway Road in no time, and then into Copenhagen Fields where the London brothers should 'ave a camp fer us. And not too far from where my brother lives, sure as I'm Johnny Devlin,' he added.

'With something to eat?' asked Joshua anxiously.

The lack of welcome they had received in the last few days had been matched by a lack of food. The porridge oats they had been generously given by the Nottingham Chartists were exhausted, and Joshua felt desperately hungry. He hoped the London Chartists would be generous.

Gradually, the leaders of the column, including Jess and Frank Mather, began to reassemble the jumbled crowd of marchers back into a column. Judd Ackroyd, with his sledgehammer now slung with a rope across his back, and Eric Naylor had been carrying the charter on a pole slung between them.

'Mr O'Connor wants it up now, lads,' said Jess. ''E's gone ahead, but 'e said we should be sure to let people know what we're about.'

As the banner went up, some kind of order was restored to the column, and the leaders asked the turnpike keeper to open the gate. The normal charge was a penny per head, but the sheer press of numbers, the resentful look on many of the marchers' faces, and the sledgehammer on Judd's back, caused the keeper to forget his toll. Opening the gate wide, he let the column of three thousand flood down Highgate Hill towards London.

This downhill stretch of road, with fine houses on either side, was welcome to Ruth and Joshua. After a hundred yards, they saw on the left a fine new building with clean stones and a large garden in front of it.

'That's the new Whittington almshouses,' said Johnny Devlin, looking down at Ruth and Joshua. 'If yer lucky enough to get in there when yer old, you'll be all right for the rest of yer life. And 'oo do yer fink they're named after?'

The children looked blank.

'Never heard o' Dick Whittington?' said Johnny.

'Oh, 'im wi't cat!' said Ruth, dimly remembering a story her grandmother had told her. 'Didn't he become Lord Mayor o' London?'

'Sure enough, that's the one,' said Johnny. 'Remember the story? 'E 'eard the sound of church bells and a voice said to 'im, "Turn again, Whittington." Well, this is where 'e turned – look at that stone.'

Ruth and Joshua stopped and looked at the engraved stone by the side of the road, marked simply:

TO SIR RICHARD WHITTINGTON

THRICE LORD MAYOR OF LONDON

1821

'Well, 'e was lucky enough in London,' said Johnny. 'Thanks to 'is cat, 'e grew so rich 'e could even lend money to King Henry V, *and* there was enough left over to build these almshouses five 'undred years later.'

Joshua began to wonder if he should be staying in London instead of returning to Todmorden. But then he had no cat; and the hungrier he became, the more he could smell his mother's oatcakes.

Sensing Joshua's thoughts, Johnny added:

'Well, it's not everyone can make a fortune. We'd best keep our place.' And the three of them rejoined Marion and Jim in their row several paces ahead.

Now the column marched southwards down a well-gravelled road which continued to slope gently towards London. Shops and houses stretched for most of its length, although there were gaps between them through which they could see meadowland on which cattle grazed. Many of the householders and shopkeepers had stepped onto the street to see the column, still over three thousand strong, march down the road.

'Well, the citizens of the 'olloway Road have never seen anything like this,' said Johnny. 'They've seen stagecoaches with thirty folk on board, and flies drawn by fine bay 'orses, sometimes a column of soldiers going up north, and even an 'ighwayman or two, but never a crowd of this size fighting for their rights.'

Joshua and Ruth felt uneasy again as they saw the

looks of fear and dislike on the faces of the people who stood in small groups along the street.

'Don't worry,' said Johnny, 'we'll be welcome enough when we get to the Copen'agen Fields where our London friends should've turned aht fer a welcome.'

As they approached the Nag's Head public house, the column turned right off the Holloway Road and onto a rougher track between hedgerows running between fields. Here too there were many cattle grazing on each side of the road.

'These are Laycock's cows,' said Johnny. 'They say he's got five 'undred if he's got one. And the milking maids to go wiv it!' he laughed. 'You've only got to walk over to Laycocks's barn over there,' he said, pointing east, 'and you'll find enough milk being sold fer 'alf of London. And old Laycock's rich enuff, that's for sure – though not as rich as Whittington, and I doubt there'll be many memorial stones to 'im.'

But the herds thinned out as the column marched further down the track and passed by a large white building with porticos and bay windows.

'And is that a lord's house?' asked Joshua.

'Blimey, no!' said Johnny. 'It's full of poor Scots women and children who can't afford the fare back to Scotland. They call it the Caledonian Asylum – that's a funny name fer the Scots' asylum and that's why this is the Caledonian Road.'

'And 'ow do they get in there?' asked Ruth, unsure if it was for good or bad people.

'Well, their fathers 'ave to 'ave died fighting Bonaparte at Waterloo or firing a cannon for Nelson at Trafalgar.'

'An' are there many of them?' she continued.

'Well, a good two 'undred,' said Johnny, 'but the mothers are beginning to die off now, and they throw the children out when they're twelve and the mothers 'ave gone.

But look over there – that's Copen'agen 'ouse, where you can get a damned fine beer – and the road going down to King's Cross.'

By this time, the column was filing off the road and onto a rough grass field lying between the Caledonian Asylum and Copenhagen House. At one point in the field there was a flagpole flying a three-coloured green, black and orange flag, with smoke that seemed to be coming from cooking fires. Now the column broke up again, and those at the front rushed forward towards the smoke.

Sensing the possibility of food, Ruth and Joshua rushed forward, leaving Johnny well behind. But Marion had not been far from them as they marched along talking to Johnny, and she now caught up with them in the rush to the cooking fires. Her short stature helped her to squeeze with the children through the ranks of marchers as near to the fires as possible.

Suddenly she and the children found themselves facing
a line of wood fires with cooking pots hanging over them.
Each fire was being tended by women with rough woollen
dresses; it was hot work and their faces were running red.
For the most part, they had been there for more than five
hours, but it was a cold day and it had taken a long time to
collect the wood for the fires. The stews they were cooking
were not yet quite ready, but the marchers were looking
down at them, hungry and impatient.

Eric Naylor was amongst those at the front, within
earshot of Marion, Ruth and Joshua.

'What's in it, love?' he cried. 'A love potion or a
good London stew?'

The cook nearest to him ceased stirring her cauldron
and looked up. 'What's in 'ere is best we can cook and
most we can afford!' she shouted.

'Well, if it's best tha' can cook, I'll 'appen try me
luck down 'ere,' said Eric.

At that, she threw her big wooden spoon at Eric,
who watched in disgust as the lumps of fatty gristle slid
down his jerkin. He picked up the spoon and began to
draw it back behind his head, just as Marion dashed in
to hold his arm from behind.

'Now then, Eric; none o' that, lad. Tha' should be
grateful for what this lass is doing. Keep quiet and wait
thy time.'

'Thank you, sister,' said a voice from across the fire.
Marion took her eyes off Eric and saw coming towards

her a woman who was about four inches taller than her, with short-cut black hair, a pale face and horn-rimmed glasses. Her hand was stretched out to shake Marion's as she said:

'That was quick of you. Chartist men will pick a fight anytime. You've got to be careful. I'm Susanna Inge, Secretary of the Female Chartist Association of London. Why don't you come round and help us with the cooking – *and* keeping the men in order.'

'Well, a' didn't come to London to cook, but I'll give thee a hand, lass,' said Marion. Turning to Ruth and Joshua, she added: 'An' you two 'ad best come too. Tha' can always stir a pot.'

They spent the next three hours with Susanna Inge moving up and down the line of twenty fires, helping to stir pots and making sure that hungry marchers did not quarrel with the cooks. Once he had been given a big ladle and responsibility for a pot, Joshua quickly found ways to quietly fill his belly. Ruth was happy enough to wait her turn and preferred to listen to Susanna and Marion. Ruth thought of Marion as being completely fearless because she always spoke her mind. But Susanna seemed to be not only fearless but to know everything there was to know about the Charter, who was fighting for it and what Parliament would think about it. In particular, and to Ruth's amazement, she seemed to be questioning whether Feargus O'Connor was the best leader the Chartists could find.

As they moved from one cooking pot to another, Susanna gave Marion her views on the problems the Charter's supporters found in London.

'London's not one place, you know. There are lots of little Londons. Villages really, like Islington – that begins with those buildings over there – or Camden – that we'll march through a bit of tomorrow and where lots of Irish live – or Kensington – where the lords and ladies who live off the rest of us live. Some people in London are doing well enough, and some people are doing damned badly. But the ones who are doing badly don't all know each other. They're in different trades and different boroughs and we can hardly bring them together, never mind reach agreement on what to do.'

'And what made thy father a Chartist?' asked Marion.

'Well, my father's a printer in Soho Square, and because he's a good one, he's usually had plenty of business. But whatever the state of his business, he's always printed for the radicals – whether it's been for the Reform Bill, or against the Poor Law, or against transporting the Tolpuddle Martyrs to Australia. And since we live above the printing shop, I've been folding and binding his printed papers since I was six years old. And I've read nearly every one of them since I was twelve – and that's a good thirteen years ago. But what with Lord Liverpool, the Duke of Wellington and our books and papers being carried off at midnight, it's a dangerous business. So I know enough to know you've got to fight them tooth and nail. Nobody will give us the Charter – I wouldn't be surprised if they won't even let the petition into Parliament.' Here she broke off. 'Will you help Jenny over there, Marion? It looks like her pot's about to fall over.'

By the time Marion returned, she was ready to hear more. Susanna carried on as she surveyed the line:

'But it's not just the government that won't listen to us. I'm worried that our own leaders might be bought off. You must have heard O'Connor speak. Just watch him carefully again tomorrow. He loves the crowds and the way they cheer him. Make him a government minister, with another kind of power, and I wonder what he'd use it for?' She laughed. 'Not for women, anyway, I'll be bound. When the Charter says, 'Universal Suffrage', he thinks it means votes for men only. How dare he? Don't we know as much as them? Don't we carry as many burdens? More, I'd say.'

Marion had never thought about that. She had somehow trusted the men to do the best they could for everybody – women and children included. The right to vote was a new prospect, which sounded better and better as she thought about it. 'That'd be grand, Ruth, wouldn't it?' she said. 'But by the time it comes, we'll probably both be grandmothers.'

'Why should you be?' said Susanna. 'That's why we've founded the FCA – Female Chartist Association. Not just to cook dinners for all these men but to fight for our rights too.'

Marion was amazed not only at Susanna's free thinking, but also at her efficiency as an organiser of both Chartist associations and of cooking pots. By four o'clock in the afternoon, nearly all the marchers had been fed and the fires were being allowed to die down. As Susanna became less busy, she began to speak less and had more time to listen to the story of Marion and the children's trek from the north.

She was delighted to meet Jess Midgeley when he came looking for Ruth and Joshua.

In his usual straightforward way, he said: 'We're right grateful to you, Miss Inge, for what you and your friends 'ave done. We'd none of us 'ave eaten today without you.' Susanna smiled.

'An' what's the plan, Dad?' said Ruth.

''Ave we got to listen to more speeches?' asked Joshua.

'No, you might get off that, lad,' said Jess. 'We'll 'ave to camp 'ere tonight, and then early tomorrow there'll be a mass assembly 'ere wi' London lads and…'

'Dad, 'ow can tha' talk o' lads when tha's just been fed by Susanna and 'er friends 'ere?' said Ruth.

Jess looked at her in great surprise but saw her meaning.

'Oh, aye. Tha's reet enough, lass. Well, let's say there'll be an assembly 'ere wi't London Chartists. Then we'll march straight t'square outside Parliament; they say it'll take about three hour. Then there will be a few quick speeches from Mr O'Connor and t'rest. Then Mr Fielden and Mr Attwood will take the Charter and petition into t'Chamber and then that'll be it. And then we'll 'ave to think about 'ow we get the members to turn it into law and 'ow we get you 'ome.'

Susanna could see that this was too simple.

'Be careful, Jess,' she said. 'There may not be as many turn out as you expect – lads or lasses. Not everyone in London is our friend. And the police are definitely our enemy. If there's any trouble on the march, they'll haul anyone in sight off to gaol. And they may try and block us from getting into Parliament Square, in which case there'll be no meeting and you might not even get the Charter as far as the doors of Parliament, never mind inside the Chamber.'

Jess looked somewhat taken aback. 'Well,' he said, 'we'll 'ave to take as it comes. There's no turning back now.'

'Well, whatever happens tomorrow, don't worry about these two tonight' said Susanna, pointing to the children. 'I'll take them home, and you too, Marion, and they can join the march tomorrow from where I live near Soho Square. You'll be coming down Oxford Street, and that's very close to my father's printing shop.'

Jess was glad enough to know that his children would be in good hands. 'That's grand,' he said, 'an' I'm right sorry about the lasses, Miss Inge. I'll never forget 'em again.'

Ruth and Joshua couldn't believe that they were actually going to stay inside a house again, or that they might even eat a normal supper round a table. Leaving the cooking pots to be used for breakfast porridge, and after Marion found Jim to tell him their plan, she and Susanna set off with the two children. Leaving the area of rough grassland where the marchers were camping, they quickly found that the fields sloped away down towards a mass of buildings. As they came close to the bottom of the hill, they found themselves on a bridge over a canal, which was swarming with traffic.

'That's the Regent's Canal,' said Susanna. 'Named after our late King George IV when he was a regent for his mad father – and a gambler and spendthrift.'

'That's a right lot o' boats,' said Joshua.

'Carrying grain and coal, mainly,' said Susanna. The grain comes in from overseas to Limehouse Docks on the Thames and then up here and on as far as Birmingham on the Grand Union Canal. And the barges bring back coal from the north to keep London smoky and grimy – and warm,' she laughed. 'But don't go and work on one, or you'll never earn more than five shillings a week.'

Crossing the canal, they could now see that the road they were on was about to branch into a broad thoroughfare running to left and right. Scores of horse-drawn coaches, carriages, and small cabs with dark black hoods were running in each direction. Hundreds of pedestrians were walking on both sides of the road. Many of the men were wearing top hats and dark black suits; others were dressed in the rough neckties, shirts and jackets which were more familiar to Ruth and Joshua. Marion was envious of the rich clothes worn by some of the ladies, and the rustling of colourful silk dresses was music to her ears. Ruth felt that the old faded dresses worn by other women would be much more comfortable. Ruth, Joshua and even Marion felt rather lost in the huge crowd, through which Susanna was confidently making her way. In the middle of the road was a tower about twenty feet high, which had the effect of dividing the traffic.

'That's King's Cross,' said Susanna. 'Built by Edward I, one of the Plantagenet bloodsuckers, for his wife, Eleanor. This road's so busy now because Euston Square Station's only half a mile away. You'll see it in a few minutes. Now everyone is trying to go by train somewhere or other.'

They picked their way down the busy pavements of Euston Road. Susanna turned left and led the way down a broad well-gravelled street which quickly came to a rough open square. Although surrounded by tall terraces of houses built from light brown brick, the square seemed to be an oasis of grassland and shrubs amidst the noisy streets.

'Oh, this is nice enough,' said Marion.

'Yes, nice enough,' said Susanna. 'It's Russell Square and owned by his Lordship the Duke of Bedford. He'll keep it rough like this until the price of land goes up even further – and then he'll build all over it. Just wait and see.'

They crossed the park in the middle of the square and as they came to the south side caught sight of an enormous rectangular building built in sandy stone of a completely different complexion to the brick houses of the square.

'Well, that's something useful anyway,' said Susanna. 'The British Museum – that's where they're collecting ancient things from all over the world. What's more, anyone, like you and me, can go in there without paying a thing. Even a government made up of Chartists couldn't do better than that! We'll walk round the front – it's even grander, used to be part of a lord's house.'

It was now close to six o'clock, and as it became darker and they walked down the street, west of the museum, they passed a lamplighter lighting one of a series of gaslamps that seemed to stretch as far as they could see.

'Well, we never saw owt like these lights in Manchester,' said Marion. 'Tha's got to see there by lights o' mill windows.'

'Where children never cease working,' said Susanna knowingly. 'Now we're coming out of Russell Street and into Oxford Street.'

Here, the gaslamps seemed to be even more frequent and to burn even brighter, illuminating a street which stretched further than they could see. Every second building appeared to be a shop, and Marion and the children marvelled at the fine clothes and leather goods which dominated the window displays. Susanna led them for about five minutes down the bustling street and then turned left down a street only wide enough to take a single coach. It was only dimly lit with two lamps, and they had to press themselves against the side of one of the houses lining the street as a coach and four horses sped past them.

In another hundred yards they found themselves in a better lit, pretty square with flowers and shrubs in the centre. Pointing across to the west of the square, Susanna said:

'That's us. Inge and Sons, Printers. Sandwiched between the piano makers and linen drapers. And they'd be glad to be rid of us, I can tell you. They don't like some of what we print. I mean the radical stuff. They think it's bad for their business, seeing the kind of rich customers they have. Come on, let's go in.'

She led the way to the door of Inge and Sons and, pulling it open, greeted a middle-aged man with glasses, dressed with an inky apron tied round his waist, who was pulling the levers of a large printing press. Three oil lamps lit the room. The machine hissed as the printing blocks were raised over the paper and clattered down with a bang on the reams of paper. He looked up as he saw them enter but waved them on.

'That's my father; you'll see him later,' said Susanna, picking up one of the oil lamps and leading the way through a door which opened onto a flight of steep wooden stairs. At the top they found themselves in a comfortable but simply furnished room, with a small table in the centre, a sofa and one easy chair, and a desk full of tidily stacked papers against the window. Marion noticed several copies of the *Northern Star*.

'This is where we live,' said Susanna. 'There's nobody else here. Mother died about five years ago and I manage this house myself, as well as working with father in the shop.'

'What about the Sons bit in Inge and Sons?' asked Marion.

'Well, it's my father that's the son. I've got no brothers,' said Susanna.

'So shouldn't it be Inge and Daughter?' said Ruth.

'Of course it should,' said Susanna. 'You're getting the idea now. Whether Father would have it, I don't know; but the customers wouldn't like it. Not even the Chartists. Can you imagine Mr O'Connor having the *Northern Star* printed at Inge and Daughter? That would be the day. Come on, let's go further up. I'll show you where you're sleeping.'

The top room was a kind of attic with a small window and two mattresses rolled up against the wall. Marion, Ruth and Joshua eyed them gratefully.

'Well, you two, you should be comfortable enough on those,' said Susanna. 'Just roll them out when you're ready. Now we can go downstairs and you can tell me the story of your journey. I might even write it up in the *Female Chartist* when we get it out!'

'Would tha' mind if we just went to sleep?' said Joshua. 'I don't think a can keep me eyes open another minute.'

'Neither can I,' said Ruth.

'Well, go ahead,' said Susanna. 'It'll have to be Marion that tells me your story.'

When the two children awoke the next day, it was already light. They could see that Marion was still sleeping on the mattress they had left for her. Joshua went over to wake her.

'Come on, Marion,' he said. 'Tha's got to be ready. We might miss t'march.'

'Joshua, leave 'er alone,' said Ruth. 'It'll not be seven o'clock yet.'

'An' since when did you stay in bed till seven o'clock, Ruth?'

'Well, it is summut new, I will say.'

'An' I can 'ear noise o' that printing press,' said Joshua, as they both recognised the hiss and clatter of the press on the ground floor.

'Let's look for Susanna,' said Joshua.

'You go,' said Ruth. 'I'm staying 'ere while I can.'

Joshua could find no sign of Susanna either in the sitting room or down in the printing shop where her father was at work. When Mr Inge saw Joshua, he briefly paused in his work and said:

'She's gone to give the rest of your friends their breakfast. Left before six. Said you were to join the march as it passed here at Oxford Street. About eleven.' He returned to the press.

Joshua rushed back upstairs.

'Ruth, she's gone,' he said. 'Susanna's gone. She's gone back to the camping field.'

At this, Marion woke up. 'Susanna, tha' means?' she said sleepily. 'Aye, that's reet. T'march should be near 'ere about eleven. We can join 'er group or the Tod group as they come past. So don't panic, lad. She's even left some breakfast for us. Kitchen's in t'back o' printing shop.'

'I'm off there then,' said Joshua.

'Aye, reet enough. I'll see ya there.'

After dipping heavily into the bowl of porridge which Susanna had left for them, leaving only just enough for Marion, the children ventured outside and into the square. It was a cold, bright autumn morning. There were buildings on all sides, many with large writing on the walls and with shops on the ground floor. Josiah Kirkman and Sons: Pianoforte Makers was next to the Inge Printing shop at number three. Gundry and Sons: Shoemakers to the Queen and the Queen Dowager was on the opposite side of the square at number nine. Hayes: Surgeons and Dentists was in the far corner.

The garden in the middle of the square seemed to be a meeting place for all kinds of people. Some were smartly dressed and were moving from one shop to the other. Others, in threadbare jackets and unpolished boots, were standing huddled in small groups, talking amongst themselves.

Ruth and Joshua, walking into the garden, were accosted by one of a group of six children of their own age, who were poorly dressed and looked down at heel.

'Oy, mate! Wha'cha doin'?' said the tallest of them.

'Oh, we're just 'aving a look round,' said Joshua nervously.

The boy could hear that Joshua was not a Cockney.

''Ere's one what weren't born within a mile o' Bow Bells,' said the lad. 'Wha's yer name?'

'Joshua.'

'An' the girl?'

'A'm Ruth. An' tha's right. We don't talk like thee because we're from a place in t'north.'

'An' where would that be?'

'Todmorden.'

'That's a funny name,' said the smallest boy in the group, whose features were black and so a big surprise to Ruth and Joshua

"Old on a minute, Joe,' said one of the others. 'I've 'eard o' that place.'

'In'it where John Fielden comes from, Danny?'

'Yes, that's right. You mean the one that's goin' to present the Charter to Parliament?'

'Aye, tha's right,' said Ruth. 'Mr Fielden is from Todmorden and we've walked 'ere so as 'e can present t'Charter and petition t'Parliament.'

'Well, that's good enough,' said Danny. 'We're all for t'Charter 'ere and we'll be joinin' the march when it passes dahn Oxford Street there.'

Joe spoke up again. 'We're all tailors' lads that work fer sweaters in slop shops.'

'What's a "sweater"?' said Joshua.

'An' what's a "slop shop"?' added Ruth.

'Sweaters are men 'oo get work from others 'oo are the ones 'oo've really got the contracts,' said Joe. 'They make us sweat, yer see. An' they put us to work in slop shops – not real factories. There's a lot in the cellars round the back of this square 'ere. You can't see 'em, but we can tell yer they're there all right.'

'An' 'ow long does't a work then?' said Ruth.

'Well, when we're in work, from six in the morning till ten at night, which is longer than my father worked as a slave in St Kitts, before 'e were freed and came 'ere' said Joe.

'And there's somebody who works even longer than us, Joshua,' saidRuth.

'That's when we've got work,' said Joe. 'But when sweaters 'ave finished a job, we're all aht.'

'Last July, I worked ten weeks with aht a break fer old Smithwick who 'ad bought a contract off Mason and Sons fer new liveries for the Queen,' said Danny. 'Joe and I were on the same job. We agreed to poke each other with a needle whenever we looked like falling asleep. 'Cos old Smithwick throws you aht if yer fall asleep on the job.'

'So when you're working, 'ow much does't a get paid?' said Joshua.

'Never more'n six shillin's a week, an' sometimes only four,' said Joe.

'Six shilling a week!' said Joshua. 'That's as much as me mam gets, never mind us childer. We're lucky to get one shilling and sixpence a week.'

'Well, none of us would work for less than four bob,' said Joe proudly. 'The London tailors' lads wouldn't turn up fer less, eh, boys?'

'Right enough, Joe,' said Danny. 'But what we want is not less than six. An' that's why we want the Charter. So as a Parliament elected by every man in the country can fix wages. A fair day's work for a fair day's pay – an' no sweaters.'

Ruth held her breath and just managed to restrain herself from taking on the whole group whose idea of votes for all left out half the human race. She changed the subject.

'Do you think there'll be a big turn-out for t'march?' asked Ruth.

'Yeah, probably a good ten thousand,' said Danny.

'Ten thousand!' said Joshua. 'That's nothing. We 'ad twenty thousand in Manchester, and London's supposed to be bigger.'

'Well, not everyone sees it the same way 'ere,' said Joe. 'There's twenny thousand tailors alone in London, and a good 'alf of 'em – those that don't work fer sweaters – is making eight shillin's a week. But we're all fer yer.'

'Anyway, 'ere's six that don't wanna be left aht!' said Danny. 'Let's get to the edge of Oxford Street and wait for 'em there.'

Looking at Ruth, Joshua said, 'What about Marion?'

'Aye, we'd best pick 'er up,' said Ruth. Turning to the group of boys, she said: 'We've just got to pick up our friend. We'll be back in a few minutes.'

The boys agreed to wait as Ruth and Joshua ran over to Inge and Sons to pick up Marion. Within five minutes, they were back, quickly introduced Marion to the group and set off for Oxford Street.

The street looked very different to the previous evening when the glow of the many gas lamps had made it seem welcoming and comforting. In broad daylight, it seemed much less attractive, with piles of horse dung in the centre of the road, unswept litter outside many shops and a sense of unease in the air. Some shopkeepers, fearful that the marchers might resort to violence, had already boarded up their windows. Many of them remembered the massive demonstration of 1834, five years previously, when one hundred thousand had marched from Copenhagen Fields and along Oxford Street, first to Parliament and then to Kennington Common. That had been to protest against the government's decision to transport seven trade unionists – the Tolpuddle Martyrs – to Australia to do hard labour in the outback. Although it had been largely peaceful, several shops in Oxford Street had their windows smashed as the marchers passed by.

This time, the shopkeepers had requested the Home Secretary, Lord John Russell, to provide one member of the Metropolitan Police for every shop. He had not agreed but had given orders that there should be one policeman every five yards, and that they should "arrest any troublemakers before they caused trouble".

As Ruth, Joshua and Marion, together with Joe, Danny and their gang looked up and down Oxford Street, they could see the boarded-up shops and a single file of policemen on either side of the road. Standing behind them were a mixed group of shopkeepers, spectators and supporters of the march, some of whom had tri-coloured flags in the red, green and white of the French Revolution. Looking to the right now, they could also see about a hundred yards away, a team of four horses pulling a large cart, followed by a second cart, after which a line of marchers stretched across the road.

'That's them. They're coming,' said Joshua.

'An' who'll that be in front?' said Ruth.

'I reckon that'll be Judd and Eric,' said Marion. As the carts came nearer, Ruth and Joshua craned to see whether either held the Todmorden marchers. As the first cart drew within thirty yards of them, they could see that the Charter was being held by two men they did not recognise, and behind them stood Feargus O'Connor with half a dozen others. The second cart held a huge drum with a shaft protruding on either side which Judd and Eric were holding. On the side of the drum was written: NATIONAL PETITION: ONE MILLION SIGNATURES. The petition was so huge that it had been rolled up into the drum, twice the size of a cartwheel. Judd still had his sledgehammer slung over one shoulder.

'That's them!' said Joshua, looking into the first cart.

'Ruth,' he cried, 'there's Mr O'Connor.'

As the second cart drew level with them, Ruth could not resist shouting a greeting to Judd and Eric.

''Ullo, Judd. 'Ere we are!'

Judd, more than surprised to hear his name called from the street, looked down into the group of children crowding together with Marion standing behind them. Delighted to see her with Ruth and Joshua, keeping one hand on the shaft of the drum, he slung his great hammer off his shoulder and waved it at the group.

'King Ludd 'ere'll knock a few 'eads off today!' he shouted. The boys in Danny's gang were delighted.

'Yeah, let's see you do it!' cried Joe.

Encouraged, Judd stretched out the hammer, with the big weight furthest from him, at the policeman who was standing in front of the children.

'Yeah, give it to 'im,' said Danny, as he gave the policeman a gentle push from behind.

The policeman panicked, seeing only the giant sledgehammer in front of him. Calling to his colleagues, he said:

'Arrest that man for violence against the police!'

Five of his colleagues within earshot ran towards the cart and tried to pull Judd out of it. Danny's gang ran forward and tried to pull the policemen back. Some of the officers who joined the fray dragged the children away first.

'All o' you is under arrest. Bleedin' troublemakers,' said one of the policemen, who had a finer uniform than the rest. 'Take the lot to Bow Street. Let that man go,' he said, pointing to Judd. 'We don't want to stop the march – just get it over with.'

Eric looked baffled, uncertain as to whether to jump out of the cart and defend the children or to stick to his task of holding the drum. Seeing his dilemma, Marion called to him:

'Stay where thou are, Eric,' she said. 'I'll stick wi' these.'

'That'll be difficult, woman,' said one of the policemen. 'My orders is to take these children. You'd best keep out of it.'

'Keep out of it!' said Marion. 'But two of 'em are in my charge, and their father's in't next cart.'

'That's no business of ours,' said the policeman. 'Shouldn't let his children loose in this crowd.' Turning to the eight children, he added: 'Come on, the lot of you. Bring the 'andcuffs, lads.'

Within two minutes, Danny's gang and Ruth and Joshua found themselves with handcuffs round their wrists, though their small wrists could wriggle out of them easily enough.

Seeing Joshua wriggling free, Ruth said:

'Tha'd better not, lad. Just go along with 'em for a bit.'

Marion was at a loss as to what to do as she saw the children herded together under the control of three policemen who were preparing to march them off to the place called Bow Street. Her first instinct was to dash up to Jess Midgeley, who was in the first cart with O'Connor's group. But she quickly remembered that they had nearly reached their goal. Jess should be left to complete the march, and she would wait until she could find Susanna, who would be in a much better position to deal with the London police. She stood uncertainly on the corner of the street, watching the children carried off by the police on one side and beginning to search amongst the marchers for Susanna on the other side.

CHAPTER 9

TO PARLIAMENT

The cells of the Bow Street police station were cold, damp and dark. Crouching in the corner of a cell, which also held Danny, Joe and the rest of their gang, Ruth and Joshua felt that their journey had finally ended in disaster. But it seemed as if Danny and Joe were used to prison life, and in fact they were finding plenty to joke about.

'Wondering 'ow you'll get aht, then, you two?' asked Danny.

'You might never,' said Joe. 'One o' t'gang, Lenny Riley, were put inside for stealing a pound two years ago and we've never seen 'im since – though 'is sentence were only a year!'

Ruth and Joshua looked gloomy but said little. Ruth reminded herself that Marion knew where they were and would eventually find Susanna, who appeared to know her way around every obstacle of London life. But would she really be able to get them out? And would the march be over by the time they were out?

Every now and then a big policeman came to gaze at them through the iron grille of the cell door. He carried his long truncheon with him and swung it from his right-hand wrist as he surveyed the children.

'No bleeding good, any of you,' he said. 'Pushing a policeman into a sledge'ammer's no joke. You'll not see daylight for many a month.'

'We're 'ungry,' said Danny. 'Gi' us some bread 'n' soup.'

''Ungry, are we? Well, you'll 'ave to stay that way a bit longer,' said the policeman, walking away from the cell door.

It was another three hours before the children saw him again. This time he had a key in his hand but had not left his truncheon behind.

'Well, it seems two of you might not be 'ere for long,' he said. 'There's a lawyer 'ere that wants this lady to identify Ruth and Joshua Midgeley.'

Ruth and Joshua caught a quick glimpse of the

round face of a man with little hair, spectacles and a dark top coat. To their great relief, they could see Susanna just behind him.

'Now, Susanna, which are they?' said the man with spectacles.

'Those two in the corner,' said Susanna.

'Now, you two, come out,' said the policeman.

With Danny's gang in Bow Street

'This man's a solicitor and 'e's asking for you.'

Danny and his gang were not going to let Ruth and Joshua out so easily, if they were left behind. The six of them rushed to the cell door the moment that the policeman began to open it. Ruth and Joshua were left struggling at the back, trying to get out through the door.

'Get out of the way, you lot,' said the policeman, bringing his truncheon to bear on Danny's ear. 'Clear the way for those two.'

Stung by the pain, Danny retreated, leaving enough space for Ruth and Joshua to get access to the door. As they squeezed through, they could see not only Susanna, but also Marion, who could not hold back one of her broadest smiles.

'Of all the places to 'ave to come for thee, Ruth and Joshua. Bow Street Prison in t'middle o' London!'

'Enough 'o, that,' said the constable. Turning to Susanna, he said: 'You recognise them as Ruth and Joshua Midgeley?'

'Yes, that's them; and they never pushed anyone.'

'Constable, you'll not find any evidence against these two children,' said the man with spectacles. You can tell by the way they speak they're from nowhere near London. And I'm not so sure that even the street lads of Soho are worth a magistrate's time.'

'You'll not get them out too. I saw them push one of our men into that sledgehammer. Could have smashed 'is face. Since our orders is to 'arrest any troublemakers before they cause trouble', you can say we might 'ave arrested 'em even before they attacked the constable – just looking at 'em, you can see the type they are.' He banged the door shut again as soon as Ruth and Joshua had squeezed out. 'You can 'ave those two then, but you'll not get more. Now come and sign for them at the desk.'

As they followed the constable up the dripping staircase which led to the ground floor of the police station, Ruth and Joshua held Marion's hands tight. They felt the warmth in her grasp and sensed her relief that it had been possible to prise them out of the prison cell. At the big oak desk by the door of the police station, Susanna and the lawyer signed a leather-bound book recording the fact that they had appealed for the release of the children.

As they stepped into the busy street outside, Marion said: 'We've missed best part o' t'march searching for you two. It took me a good hour to find Susanna in that lot, and then she 'ad to look for Mr 'Orniman 'ere in 'is office.'

Susanna looked serious. She had spent many hours preparing arrangements in support of the marchers and was deeply disappointed not to have been with them along the route which took them down Regent Street, across Piccadilly, into Trafalgar Square, through Whitehall and into Parliament Square. Mr Horniman looked at his watch.

'Just three o'clock,' he said. 'If you walk fast you might catch the meeting in Parliament Square.'

Susanna looked dubious.

'I'll tell you what, Susanna. I'll buy you all a cab ride.'

Bow Street Police Station was just opposite the great Covent Garden theatre, and the area in front of the theatre was a favourite place for drivers of hansom cabs to water and rest their horses. Mr Horniman shouted 'Cabbie' and one of the drivers flicked the reins of his horse and drove his black hooded cab over to where Susanna, Marion and the children stood outside the police station.

'Here, take these four to Parliament Square,' said Horniman as the cab drew up.

The driver, whose bearded, weather-beaten face made him appear remarkably unfriendly, looked doubtfully at the children and Marion. There were not many people dressed so roughly who took hansom cabs. But seeing the shilling piece which Horniman offered him, he waved the party into the cab. Susanna and Marion gave their heartfelt thanks to Horniman and leant back in the cab as it drew out of Bow Street, away from the theatre and through the narrow streets down to the Strand.

Ruth and Joshua looked through the glass window of the cab at the magnificent white columns as the Covent Garden theatre passed from their view. Within minutes, they were driving along a street lined with wicker boxes piled high with vegetables; they caught a glimpse of men, women and children struggling under the weight of the boxes as they carried them along the street.

'Where are they all going?' asked Ruth.

'They're just moving them along to Covent Garden,' said Susanna. 'That's where all the vegetables in London are marketed. But I wouldn't look for a job there if I were you. You'd get a farthing for every box you moved; and nothing if you dropped it. Look at that young girl there.'

Susanna pointed out of the window to a girl who looked younger than Ruth who was carrying a big wicker-work basket, almost as big as herself, by two ropes looped round her shoulders. Weighed down under the weight, she looked exhausted and depressed.

'It looks like she should be on the march,' said Ruth.

'So she should, but these Covent Garden people are not organised. They make a shilling a day and think they're doing well. But don't worry: we'll have a Female Chartist Association here before long.'

As the cab passed alongside the covered market at Covent Garden, the children could see a series of bays and porticoes between which vegetable and flower stalls were set out. The business of the market seemed to spill out into all the neighbouring streets, and the cab driver was shouting almost continuously to force his way through the crowd. Finally, the crowds in the streets thinned out and the cab was moving downhill into the Strand. Although this broad street was busy, the cab traffic was moving along it easily and their cab quickly reached the edge of Trafalgar Square. Here, Ruth and Joshua were amazed to see such a vast open space with a column, apparently half built, in the middle.

'What's that?' said Joshua.

'It's a column that'll one day have Lord Nelson on top of it,' said Susanna. 'But no one knows when. Parliament only voted for enough money to build it half way, and we don't know when they'll vote the other half, so the great Admiral'll have to wait.'

'Oh, you mean Nelson that won Trafalgar?' said Joshua. 'Yes, I've 'eard about 'im from Jethro.'

'Well, Trafalgar was one battle Jethro wasn't at,' said Marion, 'but I expect 'e knows all about Lord Nelson.'

The cab cut round the edge of the square and turned left into Whitehall. Suddenly they could hear the murmur of an angry crowd. The driver reined in his horses, calling down from his box:

'I'll go no further. There's trouble down there in Whitehall. Those damned Chartists are taking on the police. You'd better be walking from here.'

'What, after taking that shilling, you're too scared to finish the job?' said Susanna. 'If you cabbies knew what was good for you, you'd be handing in the Charter yourselves!' said Susanna. 'But we've no time to argue. Come on, let's run!'

Susanna jumped out of the cab with Marion and the children close behind. Ruth just had time to see that they were in a broad street full of grand buildings. On the right-hand side, outside a building with porticoes, there were a good fifty guardsmen in scarlet cloaks mounted on enormous black horses.

'Horseguards,' said Susanna. 'Nice uniforms but sharp swords.'

They looked like statues, but Ruth immediately thought of the galloping column which had trampled over Jethro at Nottingham, and shuddered. The noise coming from the end of the street was getting louder, and it too reminded her of the noise and confusion which she had witnessed as the cavalry arrested her father and the other leaders on that terrible morning. Now, as they ran down the street in the direction from which the noise came, she could see members of the crowd breaking away from it and being chased by men in blue uniforms on horseback.

'Looks like mounted police,' said Susanna. 'Dangerous and no discipline.'

At a command from their officer, the statue-like horse guards mounted on the black horses, who had been quite motionless, fanned out across the street. The group of twenty who had broken away from the crowd were suddenly trapped between the truncheons of the blue-coated policemen and the sabres of the scarlet-coated guards. Ruth reached for Marion's hand and held it tightly as Joshua pressed close to Susanna. They saw the horse guards point their sabres downwards as the twenty fugitives from the crowd were forced into a small circle, staring with anger at the horsemen who surrounded them.

Ruth, still trembling with her memories of Jethro's fate, held Marion's hand ever more closely. Suddenly she screamed:

'Don't do it, don't do it!'

Amazed at the strength of her own voice, she buried her face in Marion's shawl, as Marion held her to her breast. Deaf to the world for the next few minutes, when she opened her eyes again it was to see a familiar tall figure in a green suit looking attentively at her and Marion. Behind him, the scarlet horseguards were still strung across the street, but they had made a space through which the twenty fugitives from the crowd were being herded by the men in blue uniforms.

'Well, at least they took some notice of you this time,' said William Steele, as he scrutinised Ruth and Marion closely before turning to Joshua and Susanna.

'I don't believe I've had the pleasure,' he said, doffing his top hat in the direction of Susanna.

'Susanna Inge,' said Susanna simply.

'Best Chartist we've met,' said Marion. 'She's already cooked a meal for three thousand and rescued Ruth and Joshua from prison. But what's 'appening 'ere? We've come for t'presentation to Parliament.'

'You're just half an hour too late. This was an orderly crowd and a fine procession. For the most part, even the police behaved themselves; that is until now. The carts carrying the Charter and the petition drew up in front of Parliament just over there. A man with a sledgehammer, that I believe I've seen with you, was carrying one end of the petition. John Fielden and Thomas Attwood came out to receive them on the steps outside the House, and took the whole roll in, promising to ask the Speaker if he could lay it out on the floor of the House this afternoon. So your march has ended – but you can't escape your friends,' he said, smiling.

Ruth glanced towards the twenty fugitives who were now being herded by the mounted police down the centre of Whitehall back towards Trafalgar Square. At least their lives seemed to be out of danger. It was Joshua who took stock of the situation first.

'So it's all over?' he asked, not sure whether to be relieved or disappointed. He had always imagined that the presentation to Parliament would be dramatic and that he would be there to see it. This seemed like a poor reward for so long a journey. On the other hand, the excitement of being reunited with his father, Jess, and the prospect of actually returning home suddenly overwhelmed him.

'But where's dad?' he asked. 'Can't we find 'im now?'

William Steele looked doubtful. 'There was a

terrible crush outside Parliament, and now the crowd's disappearing in all directions. The police are not just chasing them down here; they're going in all directions – into the Westminster slums, across the river to Kennington and east to Clerkenwell. Your father and his friends could be anywhere. I'd expect the leaders to break up and go different ways in a situation like this, and there's no telling which one.'

Joshua looked forlornly at Ruth, and they both looked at Marion. Susanna caught William's glance too as they both realised that they would have to find a solution.

'Well, you can certainly all come back with me,' said Susanna.

'But 'ow do we find dad?' Joshua persisted.

'An' 'ow do we get back to Todmorden?' pleaded Ruth.

'We'll be all right, lass, don't worry yourself,' said Marion, not too convinced by her own words. Suddenly she had a thought.

'Do you remember, you two,' she said with sudden enthusiasm, 'as we were leaving the big meeting in Manchester, Mr Fielden asked us to come and see 'im in London? I never thought o' that till now.'

'Didn't 'e say we might need a meal o' two?' said Joshua, remembering Fielden's face in the flickering light as hundreds of torches were extinguished.

''E did that,' said Ruth with new enthusiasm.

'Yes, I remember that night,' said William. 'Fielden

was talking to you. I went to see him at his house here a few months ago. Now let's see. Yes, that's it. Panton Street, off Leicester Square. Not far from here.'

'Well, if he's doing his job he'll be in Parliament till close to midnight,' said Susanna. 'You'd best all come back with me, and we'll call on Mr Fielden tomorrow morning. Mr Steele, will you come with us?'

'No, I've got to see this through. Although my paper's got its reporters in the House, they're depending on me to tell them what happens in the streets. I'll come to your house tomorrow at eleven and we'll go on to Fielden's. Where are you?'

'Soho Square, on the west side: Inge and Son, Printers. That is, we print everything your newspaper leaves out and most of your readers would never believe.'

'I'll be there at eleven,' he said and, with a final flourish of his hat, set off back towards Parliament.

Stepping in the opposite direction, Susanna motioned Marion, Ruth and Joshua to follow her, and they retraced their steps towards the half-built Nelson's Column.

'No cab this time,' said Susanna. 'But we'll be home in half an hour.'

'Tha's a treasure, Susanna,' said Marion. 'I'll write a song for thee – no, more important, *about* thee.'

'Well, I'm tone deaf so don't get too carried away,' said Susanna.

Although Marion's memory of John Fielden's invitation was very clear, she could not help feeling apprehensive as she stood with the children and Susanna and behind William Steele on the doorstep of the house in Panton Street. The house lay in a short street of three-storey houses, many of which were rented out to Members of Parliament and others who needed a house in London for only part of the year. She was glad she'd asked Susanna to make the visit with them. Mr Steele was considerate, but she felt out of her depth with him. For Susanna, she felt an instinctive trust.

Shortly after William Steele rang the bell, a housekeeper appeared in a black dress and a white hat. She looked kind, and Marion felt more at ease.

'Excuse me,' said Steele. 'I am here with these friends from Todmorden. They have an invitation from Mr Fielden to visit him in London.'

The housekeeper looked as if this was not the first time she had found poorly dressed visitors on her doorstep saying that they had an invitation from Mr Fielden. But she knew that in most cases the invitation had indeed been given, and that he would wish to see them.

'Very well,' she said, in an accommodating tone. 'Come in, and I'll put you in the parlour.'

Steele led the way as Marion, Susanna and the

two children followed her into a room leading off the main hallway. There was a warm fire in the grate, white wallpaper, several bookcases full of books and a sofa and two chairs.

'Yes, I remember this well enough,' said Steele. 'I talked to Mr Fielden here when the Charter was first published in London last year.' Looking carefully at the folded newspapers lying on a low table in front of the fire, he added, mainly to Susanna:

'I'm glad to see Mr Fielden hasn't changed his taste in reading habits. We've got here a *Manchester Guardian*, a *Times* and a *Northern Star*.'

'H'm. But only one of them is worth reading,' said Susanna.

'Oh, and I wonder which of 'em that would be,' said a voice with a strong Lancashire accent from behind the door. John Fielden entered the room with a gleam in his eye and a welcoming handshake for each of the visitors. Meeting him for only the second time, and the first time in daylight, Ruth and Joshua were surprised by how small he seemed: several inches shorter than their father, Jess, and a good foot shorter than Judd Ackroyd. Marion remembered him clearly from Quaker meetings, but he seemed very different here. At the meetings, he had been quiet and had let others speak. Here, he clearly wished to be seen to be in control.

'Ah, Steele; grand to see you again.' Looking towards

Susanna, he added, 'Young lady, I don't believe I've 'ad pleasure o' meeting thee.'

'Miss Inge,' said Susanna quietly. 'I've always admired you, Mr Fielden. One of the very few masters that their workpeople can count on. And as for opposing the Poor Law, you've been very courageous.'

'Well, sometimes we can muster a bit o'c ourage when there's summut as daft as that proposed. Now, who 'ave we 'ere?'

'It's Marion Rowley, Mr Fielden. An' this is Ruth and Joshua. We met you at Manchester at that torchlit meeting and tha' said we could call on you in London. Well… we've sort of got lost – that is, we've got separated from the rest of the Todmorden marchers, and the children from their dad, and we thought we best come to see if we could find you.'

'You did right, lass. An' I do remember meeting you well enough. Well, Ruth and Joshua, 'ow does it feel to 'ave marched from Tod to London? Tha's not seen the Queen, I'll be bound. But I'll tell thee that tha's done summut better – for yesterday me and Mr Attwood presented Parliament with every one of those million and more signatures. I must say the members didn't like it much, only 46 in favour and 235 against, but before so very long I believe we'll get the Charter, right enough. So tha's done right well, and we should strike a medal for you. Sit down, sit down.'

'We've made progress, Steele,' he said, 'but this Government is not minded for any more reform of Parliament and so we've got a long way to go. Were you about in the streets yesterday? What 'appened exactly? I'm not sure I believe what I read in *The Times* anymore, but let's 'ear your side.'

Steele recounted the events that had followed the handing-in of the Charter and the fact that the leadership had been completely scattered by the police and the army. He understood O'Connor had been able to meet some of the leaders late in the evening at a public house in Clerkenwell Green, but that the police had kept a close watch; and after half an hour, the meeting had been forced to disperse. They were planning a full meeting of the leadership today to decide the next move.

'Aye,' said Fielden, 'that's tricky enough. The movement's got to decide whether to stick together or disperse and meet again next year, 'appen in the spring. If they stick together, 'appen they should move out o' London. Birmingham or Manchester'd be safer.'

Fielden caught Joshua looking anxiously at Ruth.

'Nay, don't thou worry, lad,' he said. 'Whatever 'appens, thou'll be back in Tod.'

'An' what about my dad?' asked Ruth. ''E's been wi't leaders all time on this march. Me mam'll never forgive 'im if 'e doesn't come back now.'

'Well, well, we'll 'ave to see about that,' said Fielden. 'But aren't you two 'ungry? Marion, didn't I promise you an children a meal?' He rang a bell and the housekeeper reappeared at the door. 'Mrs Halstead, give our young guests a good dinner, will you. An' mark you, plenty of Yorkshire pudding.'

Fielden sat talking with Susanna and William Steele for another quarter of an hour before all of them joined the children at the dinner table in a large dining room. By the time they arrived at the table, Mrs Halstead was already offering Ruth and Joshua a second helping of roast lamb; in the centre of the table was a giant Yorkshire pudding which was half eaten. A large mirror ran down the length of the wall opposite the side of the table at which the children were eating. Marion had been almost as intent on eating as Ruth and Joshua, but as she glanced up from her plate, she was amazed to see the picture the three of them presented. More than a month of marching with inadequate and irregular food had left each of them thin and pale. Although she had tried to tidy herself before coming to Panton Street, and although she and Susanna had brushed hard on both her hair and Ruth's hair, there was no doubt that they looked wildly out of place amidst the comforts of Fielden's house.

He showed no sign of being upset by their presence at his lunch table. Sitting down, and addressing himself to Joshua, he asked:

'Well, lad, and what was the worst thing that 'appened to thee on this march?'

Joshua looked thoughtful. 'I were alreet,' he said, 'but our Ruth all but drowned on Kinder Scout. Got fair carried away by stream, would have gone over t'cliff if it weren't for Jim 'n' Marion.'

Fielden was about to ask Ruth how she had managed to fall into such a deep stream, but at that moment the doorbell rang, and he asked Mrs Halstead to go and answer it. She came back, saying:

'There's a man from Todmorden outside, sir, asking to see you. He says he's been marching with the Chartists and his name is Midgeley.'

'Dad!' exclaimed Ruth and Joshua at the same time, as they rushed from the table out of the dining room and down the hallway to the front door. Jess stood framed in the open door, standing at the top of the three steps which led up to the front door. Both children rushed up to him and threw their arms round his neck.

'What!? Here at Mr Fielden's house? I'd not expected this! I were looking for news of any of Tod marchers and 'oping to find you through them. You're well ahead of me!'

'We came 'ere asking for Mr Fielden's 'elp, and 'e's given us a right good dinner.'

'An' where were you last night?'

'Never mind last night, Dad. What about yesterday morning? We were in t'police cells.'

'Bow Street Prison, Dad,' said Ruth. 'We were arrested along with Mick, and Johnny and their friends – we were lucky to get out. It's only thanks to Susanna that we did.'

At this point Mrs Halstead reappeared in the hallway.

'Mr Fielden asks you to come into the dining room, Mr Midgeley, if you would.'

'No, I'll wait outside wi' these two,' Jess replied.

'But, Dad, we're at the table,' said Ruth. 'Aren't you 'ungry?'

'Well, I won't say I'm not 'ungry, lass, but I'm not dressed for Mr Fielden's table.'

'That you are, Dad,' said Ruth. 'Come this way.'

Ruth took his hand in hers and walked him into the dining room.

Jess had only met Fielden face-to-face for the first time on the previous day. He had been in the second of the carts carrying the Chartist leadership when they had delivered the Charter and the petition to Attwood and Fielden outside Parliament. He'd also seen him at a distance at the torchlit meeting in Manchester, and prior to that on various occasions in Todmorden. He regarded him with respect for his stand on both the Charter and the Poor Law, but could never regard the employer of a workforce of three thousand as a comrade-in-arms. However, there was no doubt in his mind that John Fielden was the working man's best friend in Parliament.

Fielden took the initiative.

'Well, Jess Midgeley, I'm glad to meet thee. Not only because tha's done so much to bring t'Charter to

London, but also because you're the father of Ruth and Joshua.'

'It's right good of you to say so, Mr Fielden. But we should thank you too for presenting t'Charter to Parliament. Without you and Mr Attwood, we might never 'ave got it there.'

'Sit down anyway, and 'ave a piece o' this joint. Now, tell us what the plans are. I 'ear there was a meeting at Clerkenwell last night. Were you there?'

'Aye, though it were short enough, since police were camped outside and after 'alf an 'our told us we'd 'ave to pack up.'

'So was anything decided?'

'Well, it were more or less agreed that London was too dangerous. Too close t'government and too many soldiers and police about. O'Connor and Lovett proposed that the leaders and as many men as will come should move to Birmingham and set up a grand convention to keep t'Charter alive.'

'That's good enough,' said Fielden. 'I'd support that.'

'But you'll not go, Dad,' said Ruth. 'Mam'd never forgive thee.'

'Well, if the lads go to Birmingham, I reckon I'll 'ave to go with 'em. We've come so far. We've got to wait till Parliament gives us a response. Wouldn't you say so, Mr Fielden?'

'Aye, that's right enough. Attwood and I will do

everything we can. There's another debate on t'Charter in three weeks. But outside pressure will be all-important in the next few months.'

Ruth and Joshua looked crestfallen. Marion came to their rescue. 'It's all right, you two. I'll go back with you.'

'And 'ow will we get back?' said Joshua.

Fielden could see that his help was needed.

'That'll not be too difficult,' he said. 'I'll give thee each a ticket on the new railway to Birmingham, and then tha' can go by canal to Manchester and on to Todmorden. I assume you'll travel with 'em, Marion.'

'What about Jim?' said Ruth.

Marion looked uneasy. Fielden looked uncertain.

'A friend of 'ers,' said Jess. 'But 'e's coming to Birmingham, Marion. Just a few more weeks – please.'

Marion could see that she had little choice if she was to retain the confidence of those seated round the table. Even Susanna seemed to be urging her to travel with the children.

'Well, that's settled then,' said Fielden. 'There'll be a train tomorrow at seven o'clock, and you can buy a ticket this afternoon.' He took a purse from his pocket. ''Ere's three guineas, Marion. That'll get you all 'ome and give you enough to eat on the way. Mind you, though tha'll get to Birmingham tomorrow, it'll be another four days to Manchester by canal and another day and night to Tod.'

The children were not sure whether they were more delighted at the prospect of travelling halfway home by train, or more downcast at the prospect of travelling without their father. William Steele broke the uncertainty.

'You know, Ruth and Joshua, you've done enough for now. You'd do well to get home for I'm sure your mother can't wait for you to get back. I'll go with you to buy a ticket at Euston Station as soon as we leave here.'

Jess looked relieved. Marion was glad enough to have the decision taken out of her hands. Susanna was sorry at the prospect of losing her new friends so quickly.

'That's good of you, Steele,' said Fielden. 'I'll 'ave to leave for Parliament now. Jess, would you tell Mr O'Connor that I would like to see 'im this evening. If 'e can come 'ere, I'd be grateful.'

Fielden rose from the table and waved his guests through the door of the dining room into the hallway. As Mrs Halstead opened the front door, both he and William Steele reached for their top hats.

'Ruth and Joshua,' he said, 'I'll say goodbye now. Tha' did right well to come 'ere, and I look forward to seeing thee again. Where do you live in Todmorden, Midgeley?'

'Oldroyd, Mr Fielden.'

'Oh, very well, then I'll know where to find you.'

'And Marion, where's thy work? Or 'as ta lost it?'

'I was last working at 'Eathcote's mill, Mr Fielden, in t'sewing shop. But that were some time since.'

'Well, I'll give thee a note to my brother James. We can always use a good pair of 'ands. Goodbye for the time being.' He raised his hat and walked down the street towards Leicester Square and Parliament.

At six thirty the next morning, the streets outside Euston Station were already thronged with horse-drawn traffic, although it was scarcely light. Giant gas lamps lit up the square in front of the station and illuminated the enormous arch which led into it. Items of luggage were everywhere: on the ground, in people's hands, disappearing into hansom cabs, falling off carts.

Susanna led Marion, Ruth and Joshua through this multitude and under the great arch. Beyond the arch lay the six tracks and platforms. As they passed through the arch, the children could see three engines, each with a row of about twenty carriages behind them. Walking down the platform, they came closer to the clouds of black smoke that belched from the engines.

'Will it be like this all the time?' asked Ruth, concerned that she might have to breathe in black smoke all day.

'No, once they've stoked up you'll be fine,' said Susanna. 'Anyway, the smoke will all get lost in that country air.'

'Let's get to the engine anyway,' said Joshua.

They walked to the end of the platform as far as the engine.

'Well, I thought it 'ud be bigger than that,' said Joshua.

'Well, it's big enough,' said Susanna. 'This will take you at more than twenty miles an hour to Birmingham. That's how you'll be there in five and a half hours. Small it may be – fast it certainly is.'

An engine driver with a sooty face and broad grin leaned out of his cabin.

'Coming with us, are you?' he asked. 'Well, you'd best get aboard or you'll find every seat gone. Open or closed carriage?'

Marion looked at her ticket. 'It says open,' she said.

'Well then, you'll have a good blow.' The driver withdrew inside his hatch.

Susanna and Marion walked a few yards in front of the children back down the platform.

'Susanna,' said Marion, 'it's been grand. You know so much. I never expected to meet anyone like you. In fact, I didn't know people like you existed.'

'Well, I have been writing to female Chartists in the north, but you're the first I've really met. You must keep struggling, you know. Don't let a good job with John Fielden put you off.'

'Will you come and see us up there sometime?'

'I'd love to – if Inge and Sons and the Female Chartists will ever let me get away. But I've never even heard you sing, Marion; and Ruth tells me that's a treat in store. So I'll come for that, I promise.'

'We'd better get in 'ere,' said Marion. 'Come on, you two.'

She pointed to an open carriage with benches mounted on a wooden flat bed, with sideboards about a yard high.

'It'll not be so warm, but we ought to get there.'

Ruth and Joshua climbed onto the carriage and sat facing the column of smoke still billowing from the engine. Marion kissed Susanna on the cheek and looked at her through eyes full of tears:

'We'll 'ave you as Chartist leader one day, Susanna, think on.'

'I don't think Mr O'Connor's quite ready to go yet,' said Susanna. 'But I know we'll get there one day.'

By this time, the noise on the platform was intense as the engine blew its hooter and the carriages filled to bursting. Marion, like most other passengers, felt the train might leave without her if she did not get on board now. With a final wave to Susanna, she stepped onto the carriage, taking a seat between Ruth and Joshua and placing one of her arms round each of them. Susanna watched them as the train moved forward very gradually, and she waved goodbye as they pulled beyond the platform.

Ruth and Joshua waved back, but soon looked ahead to the space opening up before and around them. Within minutes they had recrossed the canal, which they had seen for the first time three days ago, and watched the buildings slip away as the train ran through the green fields surrounding Camden.

'Well, it's green all right, Joshua,' said Ruth.

'Green, but not green like a moor,' said Joshua.

CHAPTER 10

BACK TO THE MOORS

It was Joshua who saw the green of the moors first.

'Wake up Ruth; wake up, Marion,' he cried as their canal barge, the *Esmeralda*, was pulled by its massive workhorse into the Warland Basin, where barges could tie up for a day or a night.

'It's the moors, our moors. We're nearly 'ome.'

Ruth and Marion put their heads out from under the blankets which Mrs Oldcastle, the bargee's wife, had given them when they left Manchester on the previous evening. It was November now, and it had become colder and colder as they had been drawn north of Birmingham on the Trent and Mersey Canal, eventually joining the Bridgewater for the link to Manchester. They had spent much of the five days of that journey huddled round the brazier which the bargee kept alight close to the tiller. Ruth and Joshua found that they could also keep warm by running along the canal bank ahead of the barge and waiting for it to catch up. Out of a desperate need to fight off the cold, Marion had finally joined them. Where there were locks to be opened and closed, the three of them had learned to do it by themselves. At night, Marion had kept the children and the bargee and his two children entranced as she sang every song she knew, and many twice over.

They had arrived in Manchester early one Saturday morning, coming into the Castlefield Basin, close to Deansgate, where massive warehouses towered above them on all sides, and a good hundred barges lay ready to take in or unload cargo. Some of them were offloading in tunnels under the warehouses where lifting gear carried the cargo up to five storeys above the water level. There were several public houses on the quays, which were doing good business even at this time of the morning. Groups of the bargees' children were playing on the quayside.

The Castlefield Basin provided a junction between the Bridgewater and Rochdale Canals: from here nearly fifty barges a day set out for Rochdale, Todmorden and Hebden Bridge. The bargees were glad enough to carry extra passengers: they were paid by the tonnage moved, and passengers were extra unrecorded income. But there was no room below the deck; and when barges travelled by night, passengers had to sleep as best they could on the deck.

So Marion, Ruth and Joshua had been only too glad when Mrs Oldcastle, who had come down to the basin to see her husband leave, had liked them enough to lend them three blankets for the overnight journey.

'Them childer'll be shot through wi' cold in them jerkins, if that's what you call 'em,' she had said to Marion on the canal bank. 'An' I don't think much o' that shawl o' yours. Just tell that lad to follow me and I'll get tha' summut that'll warm thee.'

Joshua had followed her a few hundred yards down the towpath and had picked up the blankets that had kept the cold at bay as they travelled through open country into Rochdale and on to the Pennines. The barge's load was booked for Todmorden and so they had only stopped once – after midnight – at Rochdale for the horse to be watered and fed. Ruth had stayed awake to make sure that the horse was as well fed as he deserved, and had then fallen into a deep and dreamy sleep. It was the companions of the journey that came back to her in her dreams that night: Davey and Jack, who had tried to steal their cheese but had turned into friends; Enoch and Shep, who had guided them over Kinder Scout and then tried to slip away unnoticed in Matlock; Ellie and Mick in Nottingham, who had kept them out of danger; Joe and Danny, who they had left in a London prison; and Susanna, who had shown her a new way of thinking.

'Joshua! I were dreaming, lad,' she cried. 'Did you 'ave to wake us?' But then she looked about more carefully. 'You're right,' she said. 'We're 'ome. Marion, we're 'ome. I don't believe it. We'll see mam today.'

Marion too raised the corner of her blanket and looked out to see the dry stone walls running up the fields that rose steeply from the canal bank. Looking to the horizon beyond the fields, she could just see the gnarled and worn shape of a rock about six feet high.

'Aye, that's grand, and, look, there's the Basin Stone,' said Marion. 'I've been there many a time of a Sunday. Once I even sung there. We'll go there together soon. 'Ere's a lock. Joshua – tha'd best get out and give 'and to Mr Oldcastle.'

Joshua took the lock key from Mr Oldcastle, jumped onto the bank and ran ahead to open the lock gate. The level of the canal fell rapidly here, and there were eight more locks to be opened before they arrived at the one closest to the centre of Todmorden. Joshua, Ruth and Marion took turns to open the locks for the bargee. In the case of more than half the locks, there were barges travelling in the opposite direction, and the *Esmeralda* was obliged to wait for them while moored to a capstan well clear of the lock gates. The children found it almost impossible to be patient as the barge crawled fitfully at a snail's pace on their passage home. They pressed Marion to let them run ahead and abandon the *Esmeralda*, but she was in less of a hurry and wanted more time to think about Jim.

Jim had come to Susanna Inge's house in London the night before Marion and the children left by train. He and Marion had walked out into Soho Square and he had told her that he had decided to go with Jess Midgeley and the rest of the Todmorden marchers to join the Chartists in Birmingham.

'But Jim, lad, 'aven't you, we, all of us, done enough now?' Marion had said. 'What more can we do? Nowt'll come out of going to Birmingham. Government'll just forget about Charter. Tha' can see it 'ere. London's not Manchester. It's different, but it's where we're ruled from. Besides, I'll miss tha', Jim.'

'Will tha', lass?' he said, looking at her and pretending to be surprised. 'Well then, I'll not be long. Gi' us a month more an' I promise you tha'll not miss us again.'

'A month and no more,' Marion said. 'Or you'll be sorry you ever ran off from Arkwright's mill.'

'No, I'd never regret that, even if it was only to 'ear you sing once.'

He had left her to join the other marchers, who were camping close to Copenhagen Fields, but not before they had kissed each other under the gas flares of the square. As Marion thought about him now, she wondered whether he would be back just as he had promised, or would the wanderlust which had taken him from Derbyshire, to Manchester and on to Todmorden, keep him away from her? Deep down she felt he would be back – but that she wouldn't mention him to her mother when she saw her.

By the time the barge had pulled within sight of the Fielden Brothers' five-storey mill at Waterside, Marion was able to put her thoughts of Jim on one side. She needed work and wondered if Mr Fielden had written to his brother James, as he had promised. She would go round to Fielden Brothers' mill on the next morning and see if she could speak to Mr James. Now it was Sunday and she could enjoy her homecoming.

She looked at Mr Oldcastle as he walked beside the boat, holding the horse's rein.

'I don't think I can 'old 'em back any longer,' she said with a smile.

'Oh, that's reet enough, lass,' said Oldcastle. 'I can see it too. I'll not charge thee more for leaving us 'ere, tha' knows. It'll be fair do's and tha' can leave right enough. I've opened a few lock gates in me time,' he said with a twinkle.

After a few hundred yards, the canal ran on along the back of a series of mills with fields stretching steeply upwards to the moors on the other side. After a mile there was a lock with a pathway to the cottages at Oldroyd where Ruth and Joshua lived.

'Race you 'ome?' said Joshua to Ruth.

'What about it, Marion?' said Ruth.

'Not for me, lass,' she said. 'Besides, I'll be dropping out before you, close t'Corn Mill. You go on. I'll see tha' soon enough.'

'Right then,' said Ruth. 'This is t'biggest 'ug tha's ever 'ad. I'd die for you, Marion. I really would.'

'An' what about thee, Joshua?' said Marion, laughing. 'Would t'a go that far?'

Joshua looked uncertain. 'Come 'ere, lad,' said Marion. 'If tha'll not gi'us 'an 'ug, I'll do it missel.' Freeing herself from the arms which Ruth clasped round her neck, she leaned forward and drew Joshua to her, holding him for a good minute. All they could hear were the church bells of St Mary's.

'You've done grand, both o' you,' she said. 'I'll be proud o' you till I die. Tha' can race 'ome now. I'll find thee next week.'

The two children broke free and ran as fast as their legs would carry them, along the canal, past the mills, barely seeing barges, knocking into horses, annoying men loading bales even on a Sunday. It took them just over five minutes to reach the footbridge and look up across the field as it rose towards their line of cottages with the moor beyond.

'Stop, Joshua, stop. I've 'ad enough,' said Ruth.

'Aye, let's walk from 'ere,' said Joshua. 'An' let's just look.'

They walked now up the path to Oldroyd, suddenly

noticing beauty where they had seen none before: in the cows grazing on either side, in the old well with a crack running through the stonework, in the oak tree under which the cows stood in summer, and in the three damson trees at the top of the field whose harvest would now be over. And coming down towards them now were three women with dark shawls pulled round their shoulders against the cold of the morning, each wearing a black dress, with clogs on their feet and a book in their hand.

Suddenly the woman in the middle started to walk faster so that she could see the children climbing up the path more clearly.

'What is it, Ellen?' said her neighbour.

'Why, it's them two, an' without their dad. 'Ow dare 'e let 'em come back like that, trailing by themselves to 'ouse?'

'Mam, Mam,' cried Ruth, now seeing her mother clearly. 'We're back, back 'ome.'

'Aye, 'ere we are, Mam,' said Joshua. 'Just as we said.'

'I can see that, an' where's tha' dad?'

''E'll be back, Mam, 'e'll be back,' said Ruth. 'Don't you see we did it? We delivered t'Charter.'

'You might 'ave delivered it, but when will your dad deliver 'isself back 'ere, that's what I'd like to know.'

'It'll be nobbut a month, Mam. Nobbut a month. They'll all be back: dad, Jim Knotts, Jethro, Eric, Judd. Marion's back already, came wi'us, tha'll see 'er tomorrow like as not.'

'But not Ralph,' said Joshua. 'Ralph Murphy's not back. He was a kind of… who was that bloke… Judas.'

Emily Suttcliffe, Ellen's neighbour, was an observant woman: she could see how much the children had

Reaching Home

been through, and she knew that talk of a Judas always meant there had been a struggle.

'Ellen, tha'll want to tak 'em in,' she said. 'We'll go on to t'chapel. Welcome back, you two. We'll give thanks to God for your safe return this morning.'

Emily turned away from the children and Ellen, knowing that Ellen would never show her real feelings, even to her closest friends. Her companion, Jenny Ashworth, followed her down the hill, saying simply:

'Praise God, and never leave your mother again.'

Ellen took both children by the hand and walked with them up to the gate. She dropped their hands as they each passed in single file through the style. Turning left to the cottages, she drew a key from the pocket of her black dress and opened the door. It was getting brighter and daylight flooded in through the front window, framing Cross Stone Church on the far side of the valley. She shut the door and drew the children to her for the first time, and wept for them and for Jess and for herself.

'I prayed for you,' she said, 'but I never dreamed you'd be back.'

It was mid-January and Christmas was over, but the sound of singing from the tap room of the White Hart public house was unmistakable.

'I think I recognise that voice,' said Jess Midgeley, as he walked towards the open front door of the White Hart, with Ellen, Ruth and Joshua close by him.

'You think!' said Ruth. 'You know that's Marion. I could make 'er out a mile away.'

'Well, folk don't usually sing at their own wedding,' said Jess.

'I should 'ope not. I certainly didn't, but then it wouldn't 'ave been the same,' said Ellen, with a rare flash of humour.

They crossed the threshold of the inn to find a room which was brightly lit with powerful oil lamps, with a strong smell of tobacco and beer and a good forty men and women crowded round the bar. Marion was standing behind a chair on the right-hand side of the room, leading the singing of '*Britannia's Sons, Though Slaves Ye Be*'. Jim Knotts was to her left with his arm round her shoulder.

As Joshua peered through the smoke, he could make out the figure of Jethro beating time to the music with his crutch. Rushing over to him, he cried out:

'Jethro, Jethro, you're back.'

'Aye, I am that, lad. Back from t'wars again. An' you can see a few other of your old comrades 'ere too. There's Eric and Judd.'

'So we all got back bar one,' said Joshua.

'Aye, bar one, that's right enough,' said Jethro. 'An' mark my words, when tha's got nine men in a corner, it's often enough there's one of 'em's a traitor.'

'Well, Jethro, you weren't nine men in a corner,' said Ruth. 'You were seven men and two women.'

'Right enough, lass, right enough,' said Jethro, puzzling over the truth of this.

Judd and Eric came over to join them.

'Well, well, you two; ready for the road again?' asked Judd.

'No, thanks, we're just trying to find work 'ere, Judd,' said Joshua. 'Stansfield wouldn't tak us back, and we've found nowt else yet.'

'Oh, not so lucky as Marion then,' said Eric. 'She's been takken on at Fieldens'. Five bob a week n'all. She'll be able to keep Jim in style,' he said, winking at Judd.

Suddenly Ruth and Joshua heard their names being called by Marion.

'Ruth, Joshua, I want you two over 'ere,' she said. 'I don't get married every day, and I want you with me.'

The children walked over to where Marion and Jim were standing, as Jim moved up another chair. They took their place in front of them as Marion led with the chorus that had filled the air at Ancoats as their column had marched into Manchester:

> *"With Henry Hunt we'll go me boys,*
> *With Henry Hunt we'll go,*
> *We'll mount the cap of liberty,*
> *In spite of Nadin Joe..."*

and the words came back to Ruth and Joshua as they came to the last verse:

> *"And let us not forget the day,*
> *That we held up our hands,*
> *And hope to flourish once again,*
> *All in our native land."*

Although the singing went on till midnight, Ellen took Jess and the children away within an hour. She could never be comfortable in a public house and feared that Joshua would be led astray. Jess was not in the frame of mind to argue against her. He was happy enough that Jim and Marion were together. Whatever happened to the Charter, that was one good outcome of the march. The days in Birmingham had been difficult: the leaders had quarrelled, Lovett and others had been jailed, public support had weakened; above all, Parliament seemed indifferent to the million and more signatures. He was no longer sure of the way forward. He wanted time to think.

It was a brilliant night sky as the family walked back along the canal. The canal bank was frozen, the moon was nearly full and there seemed to be more brighter stars than Ruth had ever seen. As Jess and Ellen crossed the footbridge and began the walk up the footpath, he put his hand in hers, and the children fell behind.

'An' what do you think, Josh?' said Ruth. 'Will we flourish once again all in our native land?'

''Ow should I know?' said Joshua.

'I mean Davey an' Jack, an' Eric, an' Ellie an' Mick, an' Joe an' Danny. Will they be all right? Or will they be like dad, an' Judd an' Jethro – kind of stranded?'

'I can't say, Ruth,' said Joshua. 'An' I can't see.'

Ruth looked up at the moon and looked down at its light on the frost. Smiling, and looking at the ground, she said to Joshua:

'Well, as long as there's moonlight shining on frost like that, there'll be summut worth marching for. An Charter's best thing I know. Aye. Lad?'